Julie Bozza

The 'True Love' Solution

Manifold Press

Published by Manifold Press

ISBN: 978-1-908312-80-8

Proof–reading: Zee | Two Marshmallows | twomarshmallows.net

Editor: Fiona Pickles

Text: © Julie Bozza 2016
Cover image: © Natalia Bratslavsky | iStockphoto.com
E–book format: © Manifold Press 2016
Print format: © Julie Bozza 2016
Set in Adobe Caslon Pro and Distillery Script

For further details of Manifold Press titles both in print and forthcoming: manifoldpress.co.uk

One

The best thing about working from home, Jules thought as he danced lightly down towards the front door, was ... No, strike that. The best thing about working from home was spending all day in his pyjamas. Jules laughed under his breath, and detoured to scoop up Jem's pashmina from her armchair. He slung it around his hips and fastened it with a loose knot while he sashayed through to the hall. A quick glance in the hall mirror reassured him that his quiff of thick red hair was looking rakishly mussed, and his pale face was unblemished by the remains of breakfast or random pen marks. Presentable, or enough so.

The second best thing about working from home was – No, that wasn't true either.

The *third* best thing, Jules amended as the doorbell rang once more, was that he could accept delivery of whatever little goodies might have found their way into his Amazon shopping cart that week. And completely fluster the delivery guy while he was at it.

"Hellooooo!" Jules sang as he flung the door and his arms open wide.

Sure enough, his bright smile fell on poor old Bart, their regular. "Hello, Mr Madigan," Bart said with only a hint of long-sufferingness. He handed over a large padded envelope that had DO NOT BEND stamps all over it. "Here we are, then."

"Oooh, Bart ... are you sure you don't want to bend just a *little*?"

"You'll need to sign for this one," Bart said, his tone as stoic as ever. Meanwhile, he was frowning while jabbing a finger at the keyboard of his electronic device, as if he hadn't been using it for three years already.

Jules took the thing, and scribbled something resembling his usual signature – remembering that he had to press hard on the device's screen to make an impression. "You know, darling," he confided to Bart, "you might enjoy getting in touch with your inner Alan Cumming ..."

Bart sighed. "Maybe I would, if it meant I got to wear me jammies all day."

"You would!" Jules bubbled over with laughter, he just couldn't help it. "And you know what you get to wear on your birthday, right?"

"Reckon I can guess."

"Well, *do* remember to drop by on Friday next week, so I can show you how it's done."

Bart let out a heavy breath, before pressing his mouth flat as if either suppressing a smile or making a mental note to take that day off. Probably both. "O' course, Mr Madigan," he said in completely unconvincing tones. "See you, then."

"See you then!" Jules cheerfully replied, and he closed the door as Bart retreated in good order.

The second best thing about working from home was that Jules could make his coffee just the way he liked it. He always went into the office on Wednesdays to catch up, and it was a pretty cool place, and he loved the people there – but even so, they didn't offer anything better than drip-brewed coffee, which tasted burnt as often as not, and given he was only at the office one day a week they frowned a little on excursions to Jules' favourite coffee shop. Jules wasn't in a position to indulge himself in big-ticket items, but a flash espresso machine was one of his few Home Essentials, along with a couple of cafetières for when a whole pot was required. He was just admiring the crema on his black coffee in the glass-and-stainless-steel cup when he remembered. The envelope.

His gaze snapped to it, sitting there on the kitchen table where he'd left it while distracted by the need for coffee. It was only now that he realised what it must be. He could hardly even voice the words to himself or see it in his mind's eye, but excitement effervesced through him.

Jules carefully put the coffee down on the worktop – he wasn't going to risk taking it near the envelope and what it contained – and stepped over to the table. After a moment, he stepped back again to fetch a sharp little knife from the kitchen drawers so he could carefully slice open the envelope and deal with any tape that had been used in the packaging. He could already feel that there was a stiff (ooh-er) piece of cardboard inside, keeping everything ship-shape.

Within moments, he was drawing out the contents, which were two bits of card wrapped in plastic. Jules carefully took them apart.

Sandwiched between the cardboard was a piece of A4 paper, quite ordinary except for the fact that it contained the typewritten last paragraphs of Jules' favourite novel. He hardly dared touch it, but lifted the paper along with the cardboard in order to marvel at it. After a moment, he let reverential fingertips drift across the letters, feeling the light indentations that the typewriter keys had made, the slight change in texture between the black ink and the cream paper. Feeling yet again a surge of the magic and the emotion contained in the words.

Best of all was the annotation in blue ink, where the word 'perfect' had been crossed out, and 'yare' handwritten in the margin to the right. Jules stared hard at the lettering, and let out a wondering breath. The man Himself, author Ewan Byge must have written that. Jules let a fingertip settle on the word, and gave serious thought to swooning.

By the time that Jules' father Archie and friend Jem had arrived home from work that evening, the piece of paper was safely secured within the frame that Jules had had waiting for it. Jules hadn't wanted to let the thing out of his sight, though, so it was standing at the back of the kitchen table, propped up against the wall.

"What's that, then?" Archie asked, squinting at it as he sat down in his usual place at one narrow end of the table.

"A page from a manuscript."

"Fancy frame," Archie remarked.

The frame was ornate and silver, and there was the palest rose-pink mat surrounding the page itself. "It had to be fancy enough for a wedding," Jules explained. "A *gay* wedding."

"Oh God," Jem groaned, and rolled her eyes. She always sat opposite Archie, at the other end of the table. "Here we go."

Archie glanced from one to the other of them, and took a guess. "This has something to do with your romance novels, doesn't it?"

"Yes." Jules had brought over the chicken, sage and mushroom pie he'd baked, but Jem hauled it closer to begin serving, knowing he was likely to get distracted. "Yes, this is the last page of the original manuscript of my favourite novel *ever*."

"Oh yes," Archie said. "Something about solutions ..."

"*The 'True Love' Solution*," Jules intoned, "by Ewan Byge, spelt –"

"B-Y-G-E," they all chorused, "pronounced 'bye'."

Jules narrowed his eyes at them, and continued, "It's a modern-day take of *The Philadelphia Story*, remember?"

"How could we forget?" Jem muttered. She was well into devouring her first slice of pie. Archie belatedly followed her example, while nodding encouragingly to Jules.

"Well, Tracy and Liz have just got married, and they're happily drinking champagne, and Mike sails off with Dexter in the *True Love*. That being Dexter's yacht. And they all live happily ever after, the end."

Archie peered doubtingly at the manuscript page. "Is that how it goes?"

"No, of course not! I'm synopsising. Of course Ewan Byge writes better than that. He's *amazing*. He writes *beautifully*." Jules gave a rapturous sigh. "That's the sort of love I want."

"Yeah? With Mike or with Dexter?"

Jules flashed Archie a grin for paying attention, but quibbled over an answer. "Mike, I suppose … He's a writer, too – like Ewan. But let's face it, I'm no Dexter."

"Any Mike would be glad to have you, Jewels."

"You have to say that, 'cause you're my Dad." Still, he squirmed a little with happiness, as he always did when Archie called him Jewels.

"Jules," said Jem – "Ginger Jules," she added, cutting him down to size – "eat your pie."

"All right, all right," he mock-grumbled. The mundane necessities of life demanded attention, too, he supposed.

"It's good though," Jem added, with a cheeky wink.

"It's a very good pie, son," Archie agreed.

"Thanks," Jules said, grinning again. He didn't have a Happy Ever After of his own yet. Didn't mean he wasn't happy.

"How d'you know it's even real?" Jem asked later that night. She was leaning against the door jamb, watching while Jules hung the framed page in his bedroom. He'd had the place picked out almost since he'd hit the Submit Bid button on eBay. It was on the wall at the foot of his bed, where he'd be able to look up and see it, whether he was reading or dreaming or … well, doing anything, really.

Jules pulled a wicked face at himself, and hummed enquiringly in Jem's direction.

"Mean to say, it's just some typing on a bit of paper. Anyone could have done it."

He cast a look at her. "Since when did you get so cynical?"

"Dunno. Can't remember back that far. Think I was about three?"

"Ha ha," Jules said, though he knew well enough that Jem hadn't had a great family life. That was why she'd come to live with Jules and Archie, after all.

"How d'you know it's not just a photocopy?" Jem continued.

"Ah. Because when I touched it I could feel the indentations that the typewriter keys made."

Jem tilted her head in a quibble, but let him have that one. "How d'you know, then, that someone hasn't just typed out a hundred of 'em? They're the words from the book, right?"

"Yes, except it's been edited." He indicated the word 'yare' substituted in blue ink, though he admitted to himself that could have been done by anyone as well. "And he typed 'The End', see? That's not in the book."

"But the words are just the same as in the book otherwise? So no one's, like, pretending this was a messy first draft?"

"No ... It's the manuscript he submitted to the publishers. Or it's meant to be," Jules added lamely.

Jem took pity on him. "Don't mind me, Gingerbread Jules. Too cynical, like you said. Think it's sweet, actually."

"Thanks," he said, glancing her way – though he was careful not to look closely because he was sure she was making obvious how much she pitied him and his romantic dreams. He decided to change the subject. "How's work, anyway? You haven't mentioned it much lately."

"It's fine," Jem said with a shrug – though the corners of her mouth threatened to betray her into a smile. Jem worked as a concierge at the prestigious St George hotel, and she *loved* it. "Guest turned up today with his new pet fish. Had to source a proper aquarium for him. And food. What kind of food d'you reckon a shark eats?"

"He had a pet *shark*?"

"Yep. So there was that. Also, spent the afternoon shadowed by a twelve-year-old whose nanny fell ill. Weird kid, but funny with it. Managed to prevent him seeing the lacy knickers I found tucked away behind a plant pot on the terrace. Finished up by scoring a pair of tickets to a sold-out concert at the O2."

"For yourself? What's the gig? Who're you taking?" He batted his eyelashes.

She regarded him scornfully. "For a guest, o' course!"

Jules sank again, but laughed fondly. "Always meeting people's needs, that's you. Not mine. *Other* people's."

"Always." She winked at him. "In all circumstances."

"Never heard of leaving them wanting more?" he asked.

"Mate, they *always* come back for more of what I've got."

He chortled. "Don't I know it." Not that Jem brought as many hook-ups home now that Archie had moved in with them. Jules was absolutely sure that didn't mean Archie had cramped her style any. No doubt she had a long list of alternative locations.

"G'night, Jules," she called as she headed across the narrow landing to her room.

"Salacious dreams, Jemima," he called back, as he always did.

"Cheers! And yourself."

"Who even uses a typewriter any more anyway?" Jem asked over breakfast the next day.

Jules lifted his mug of coffee to serve as both sustenance and shield, and grimaced at her. "Urgh," he remarked.

Archie looked at them both, a bit puzzled. He asked Jem, "Is there a reason why this is bothering you?"

"Know how much he paid for it, don't I?"

"Oh." Archie turned a little on his seat to face Jules directly. "How much did you pay for it, son?"

Jules shot a malicious look at Jem, and then prevaricated. "The bidding went a bit higher than I thought it would."

"Yes?"

"I'd set my heart on it by then."

"And?"

Jules sighed. "A hundred and eleven pounds fifty."

Archie sucked a breath in through his teeth. Jules could almost read his mind: 'Over a hundred quid for a piece of typewritten paper? For words that you've already read twenty times in a book?'

Times had been lean for a long while, back when Archie had first moved to London from Essex and Jules was still studying. "It's not as if I'm not earning now," Jules protested.

Jem retorted, "It's not as if you don't have to pay rent."

He bit back. "The rent is covered, all right?"

"Son," Archie said. "If it makes you happy, then I'm happy. But that's a lot of money."

"I know. Of course I know. Qualified accountant now, remember?"

"I remember," Archie replied rather heavily. And Jules didn't have the heart to argue any more.

Soon Archie and Jem had headed off to work, both taking the same Tube for a few stops before Archie changed lines. Archie was a fair bit older than most fathers with twenty-nine-year-old sons, and when he'd come to London to live with them, he was supposed to be on early retirement. But he'd found the days a bit empty, and ended up volunteering to help at an old folks' home. This had become a part-time temporary job, and they'd all liked him so much that he was now there full-time and permanent. He did things like helping the old people bathe or do their exercises or work on craft projects, and he drove the bus and pushed wheelchairs when they went out for day-trips. He did the things for which they needed strength, diligence and cheerfulness, all of which Archie had in abundance, even if he was barely a generation younger than them.

Jules had asked him once if the bathing duties squicked him out, but Archie had just shrugged. "We all get old, Jules – or should do, anyway." And Jules couldn't argue with that. Not that Jules was looking forward to turning thirty, but hey it was still a long way off seventy or whatever, so he resolutely pushed the issue out of his mind once more.

Anyway, all of that meant that the house was nice and quiet during the days. The Flatmate from Hell was long gone, and though Archie had moved in soon thereafter, he had only hung around at home for a week or two before starting his volunteer work. So, there were minimal distractions. Jules had his computer and paperwork set up in a corner of the second reception room, just off the kitchen so that the coffee was handy.

The June VAT quarter had ended the week before, so Jules spent that day checking their clients' spreadsheets and working out their VAT returns. He enjoyed the work well enough and liked making sure the figures were nice and neat, but there were only so many VAT returns you could work on before flagging somewhat in the Enthusiasm Department.

At lunchtime Jules indulged himself by Googling Ewan Byge. Jules found an article looking at 'gay marriage one year on' which he hadn't seen before. Ewan had always been vocal in support of the issue, and now he was asked when he personally would take advantage of the legislation. 'Just as soon as I find the right chap,' Ewan replied, rather reassuringly.

Jules didn't find any new news, so he tracked down the interview in which Ewan talked about his trusty old Underwood typewriter. It had been a manual machine, too, not even an electric. His publishers had eventually insisted on dragging him from the nineteenth directly into the twenty-first century, and had bought him a sleek new laptop, but he had been very fond of his typewriter. 'I'm adjusting,' he was quoted as saying. 'I hope that my writing won't.' Despite having read this before, Jules mock-gasped and clutched his chest at the thought. Jules *loved* Ewan's novels, and the thought that his publisher had potentially jeopardised Ewan's creative process was just the most ghastly thing.

But this was what made that framed typewritten paper on Jules' bedroom wall all the more precious. *The 'True Love' Solution* was the last novel Ewan had composed on his Underwood, and Jules now possessed the very last page of it. Jules could even almost understand Jem's scepticism, as it was all so perfect – almost too perfect to be true. But it *was* true – as was Dexter's love for Mike and Mike's for Dexter. Just as true as the best kind of love. The sort of love that surely Jules would find one day. The sort of love that Ewan Byge must have known in his own life, or how else could he write about it so beautifully? Even though he was always reported as being single – or as Ewan Byge Himself put it with a wink, 'available' – he must have known True Love. He must have experienced it. And that meant he must be looking for it again.

Jules sighed quite happily, and opened up the next spreadsheet.

Two

Jules' birthday began with coffee in bed courtesy of Archie, and fresh croissants from the nearby bakery courtesy of Jem. Once they'd all imbibed a few mouthfuls of caffeine, Archie went to fetch his present – or Jules should say presents plural, each of them neatly wrapped in plain paper. Archie handed them over with a "Happy birthday, son", then sat down at the foot of the bed.

The first that Jules opened was a paperback copy of the latest novel from Ewan Byge, *Sherbet and Sin*. "Ooh!" Jules quietly squealed, clutching the tome to his heart. "I only have this on Kindle. Thanks, Dad!"

"My pleasure, son. Waterstones said it had only just come out, so I hoped you hadn't got there first."

"No, it's perfect." The next pressie was a soft silk shirt, coloured a profound dark blue with huge hot pink lilies and creamy frangipani blooms bursting across it.

Archie winced a little as the shirt emerged from the plain brown wrappings. "I hope that's all right."

"Oh God, it's *beautiful*." Jules gently rubbed the silk between his fingertips, then lifted the shirt to admire the flamboyant pattern, before bringing it to his face to feel and inhale it. "The most *gorgeous* shirt *ever*, Dad."

"Told you," Jem said complacently. "Need something vivid for His Gingerness, so you do."

Jules glanced at her, but was too happy to even roll his eyes. The third present from Archie was a gift card from Amazon for thirty pounds. The card had the Kindle logo on it, so Jules knew Archie was expecting him to be buying more romance novels with it. "Oh Dad, you shouldn't have – but I'm ever so glad that you did."

"I'm glad, too, son."

Jules knelt up and tumbled over onto all fours to stalk down the bed for a hug. "Best Dad Ever."

"My precious Jewels," said Archie, enfolding him in both loving arms.

Even Jem was looking sweetly sentimental as they drew apart. She stepped closer, and handed over another present. "Happy birthday, Jules," she said.

"Thanks," he replied, grinning at her. The pressie was smallish, and box-shaped, and Jules thought it must be jewellery – a theory soon proved correct. "Oh God, you *really* shouldn't have," he murmured as he lifted out the treasure.

"Yeah, I should," she argued equably.

It was a silver charm bracelet with a difference. Instead of bits dangling off a chain, it was a series of flat panels into which were set small rectangular charms. Most of the panels were still blank, but there were three charms already: a J for Jules or for Jem, a red love heart with an arrow through it for the obvious, and a number 30. "You have to remind me?" he mumbled, without heat. Thirty years old, for heaven's sake!

"You're getting better with age, mate," she replied.

"Like a fine wine?"

"Was thinking more like cheese. The pungent stuff."

But Jules was too touched by the gift to bite back. He smiled at her, a bit wobbly. "This is beautiful. Thank you, Jem."

She came over to the bed and leant down to crush him into a hug. "You're welcome. Be interesting to see how we fill it up over the years, right?"

"Right." He grinned at them both. "God, you guys are the best and I'm the luckiest."

Archie looked fond, while Jem rolled her eyes – but her lips twitched as she suppressed a smile. "Right," Jem said, all business-like now, "time to get on. *Some* of us have to work for a living, you know."

Jules spluttered at the familiar argument. "You think I sit around all day watching daytime soaps and chat shows?"

"Hardly like to imagine *what* you watch," she commented darkly, before heading off with her trademark long-legged sauntering stride.

"Happy birthday, son," Archie said once more, stopping for another hug before leaving. "I'll bring you the cafetière," he called back as he headed down the stairs.

"I love you, too!" Jules cried in response.

It looked set to be a perfect day.

A knock on the door that morning proved to be a florist rather than Bart the parcel delivery man. Jules was rather disappointed to miss the chance of teasing Bart about wearing his birthday suit. He could hardly be unhappy, though, with the huge bouquet of pink, orange and yellow gerbera daisies that was presented to him, sent by his boss and colleagues. Which was pretty decent of them, seeing as they'd already taken him out to lunch on the Wednesday that week, in between briefings on updates to the tax laws, chewing over the implications of the Budget, and discussing the latest episode of *Humans*.

There were a few texts and Facebook messages from his friends, but otherwise Jules spent a quiet day polishing off the last few VAT returns and answering various queries from clients. Bart still hadn't shown up by mid-afternoon – which probably meant that he wouldn't now – but then an email popped into Jules' Gmail account. Usually he was pretty disciplined about ignoring his personal email during the day, but this one had an intriguing title: WRITERS MEMORABILLIA. He aimed a disapproving moue at the spelling mistake, paused for a moment's reflection about nothing much, and then clicked through to open it.

'Thank you for purchasing WRITER'S MEMORABILLIA from us recently. A number of interesting items recently came on the market, and as a connesieur we thought you'd appreciate a first look. Please note these items will go on the general market soon, so snap up a treasure while you can!'

Hhhmmm, thought Jules. He was perfectly happy with his manuscript page – the last page, the Happy Ever After of his favourite novel, his favourite fictional couple – and he couldn't see how anything could top that. But he scrolled down the page of text and occasional images, quickly browsing, just in case.

About halfway down, an image caught his eye. It was of an Underwood manual typewriter. Jules recognised it from looking up the model on Wikipedia. It was the exact model that Ewan Byge used. Actually, this was the same photo used on Wikipedia, Jules was sure, with a posed shot of the typewriter against a blank white background. He scrolled down a little further, and there was a poorly scanned copy of the magazine interview with Ewan – the page with the photo of the author standing by his desk, with the typewriter in place and a pile of blank paper beside it. (And oh my ... Ewan

Byge was just *fine* with his shaggy brown hair and green eyes and the way he cocked his slim hips as if issuing an invitation …)

Jules cleared his throat and scrolled back up again to read the text. None of it was formatted or anything. It looked as if the text had been painstakingly typed into Notepad and copied across. No nice HTML or CSS, no spellcheck even. Just the facts, ma'am. Jules wasn't very impressed. His company always made sure their own emails, forms and spreadsheets were totally correct and neatly designed. But then … Jules supposed they *were* accountants, and therefore had to convey an impression of super-duper accuracy and professionalism in order to help the client feel they could be trusted. What did a purveyor of writerly memorabilia want with all that? Well, except that surely he or she should know how to spell! This email failed dismally on all counts … and yet it was intriguing.

Jules tapped up to the top of the email and scanned through it again. The only other item relating to Ewan Byge was an autographed copy of a first edition of the first novel he'd released, *Desire and Discombobulation: A Comedy*. Jules shrugged. He already had copies of all Ewan's first editions, and he had three autographs as well – personalised ones – though two of them were on photos rather than in books. There was really only so many autographs that one fan needed …

But a typewriter … *The* typewriter.

And that was quite something when all Jules could see from other writers were signed photos, out-of-print books and related merchandise, and the occasional pen. Though he had to laugh at someone's old woolly cardigan being on offer! Jules couldn't imagine Ewan Byge being seen dead in such a thing. This was pretty ordinary stuff, from people whose names he mostly didn't recognise. Perhaps they didn't write romances.

He kept coming back to the typewriter. Jules sighed. He guessed that trumped the manuscript page … and on his birthday, too. It was almost as if it were meant to be. Didn't he deserve a birthday treat? And it was only … well. Seven hundred pounds.

Jules sighed, and closed the email. He was earning good money these days, after years of temp admin and waiting work, but that was a lot to spend on something that would just sit around gathering dust.

Another sigh. It really was a rather stupid idea. Jules opened up one last spreadsheet that had just come in for VAT return calculations.

But he didn't delete the email.

Archie took Jules and Jem out for a curry that night, to Jules' favourite Indian, where he had his absolute favourite meal of butter chicken, coconut rice and a peshwari naan. The other two were in a celebratory mood, though Jules had to admit to feeling rather ambivalent about this whole Turning Thirty thing.

"Cheer up, Gingerbread Man," Jem ended up telling him. "It's *your* day! Or, the way you celebrate birthdays, it's your whole fuckin' month."

"Yeah, sorry," he said, with a smile that was just a bit too weak.

"*Really* don't see the problem." Jem rolled her eyes. "We're livin' in *London* now. *London*, mate. We're earning some proper money at last. And Archie moved in, so we're all together again. Where's the downside?"

Jules opened his mouth but then shut it again without saying anything. They all knew what he wanted in his life, after all.

Archie gently grasped his shoulder for a moment. "It'll happen, son. You're the most loveable person in all the world, I reckon. One day someone else will see that, too."

"When?" Jules asked with his whole heart and his gut yearning to know, though his head knew there could be no answer, not even from his father who was wise in all kinds of ways.

"I don't know, son. But keep believing. You never know what might happen …"

And there was a glint of a secret waiting to be told in Archie's warm brown eyes, but just as Jules was about to follow up on that, the waiter came to clear their plates and ask them about pudding and coffee, and the moment was lost.

Archie headed home soon after, leaving "you two youngsters" – "Ha!" Jules had scoffed – "all right, my precious Gem and Jewels" to go out clubbing.

Jem knew all the best places, of course. The places that flew the flag for the whole spectrum. Sooner than even Jules could imagine, she'd slipped away into a dark corner with someone – boy or girl or otherwise, Jules didn't see and Jem didn't care – so Jules lost himself in the crowd on the dancefloor.

He was happy enough just to be dancing, to be feeling the beat groove through him and the melody lift him. After a while, a fellow dancer, a guy with a sweetly risqué smile, began displaying dishonourable intentions towards Jules, and Jules was happier still. He had never been backwards in such situations, so he threw his best moves and strutted his best stuff, before easing close and teasing this prospect with the potential of a kiss …

They were just about to put the matter beyond doubt when, with the most appalling timing, the first edgy chords of 'How Soon is Now?' blasted from the sound system – and Jules maintained a Stiff Upper Lip for the start, but he could hardly help weeping by the heart of it, which of course scared the other guy off, and who the hell could blame him? Damn it!

That didn't help the stupid tears, and even his frustration and his anger at himself only made his eyes wetter still. Jem found him well before the end of the song, and took him into her arms, and they slow-danced even when the songs returned to a more frenetic beat.

"All right?" Jem eventually asked him, murmuring in his ear. He felt the vibrations as much as he heard the words.

"Yeah, I'm fine. Might call it a night."

She nodded. "Of course. We'll head home."

But Jules had known her for too long, and could read the slight dash of disappointment. "Nah, you stay. Don't worry about me."

Jem scrutinised him, and Jules knew she could read him as well as he could read her. Nevertheless, she asked, "Are you sure?"

"Absolutely. I'll be fine. I've got a couple of new novels on the Kindle!"

A doubtful look crossed her face, but she didn't argue. Instead she leaned in to press a warm kiss to his cheek. "G'night, Ginger Man."

"Salacious adventures, Jemima!"

"Cheers." And with a bold grin and a wink she slipped away through the crowd.

Jules sighed and turned towards the exit. Within moments he was out in the fresh cool night air, striding towards the nearest Tube station. If he was in luck, he would make it all the way home without having to rely on the night bus.

There was too much time to reflect during his journey, of course. He'd often tried to adopt Jem's more casual approach to hook-ups, and it wasn't as if Jules hadn't achieved exactly that a hundred times before. Why he'd let it go so utterly pear-shaped this time, though, he had no idea … Unless it was the sneaking suspicion that it seemed a bleak way to celebrate his thirtieth birthday, when really he wanted so much more. Could it be that obvious? Could he be any more pathetic than right now, alone when he had no real need to be … ?

Jules sighed.

When he finally reached home, he let himself in quietly. Archie had left the hall light on for them, but the rest of the house was dark and quiet, so Archie must have settled for the night.

Jules headed upstairs, and slipped off the beautiful silk shirt his father had gifted him, the gorgeous charm bracelet from his best friend, his sister-by-choice. He already had so much good in his life, so much more than many people he knew. His gaze strayed to the framed manuscript page, and he smiled a little wryly over Dexter and Mike's happy ending. Jules already had so much. But Jules' gaze wandered towards his laptop, and he thought about that email.

It was his birthday. Why the hell shouldn't he treat himself?

Three

Jules was going to be a bit clever about this. He replied to the email before he went to bed, expressing a cautious interest in the typewriter. 'But is that really the actual typewriter in the photo?' Jules asked, being a little disingenuous. Or maybe a lot. 'It looks like it's a hundred years old!'

The reply arrived the following morning. 'Yes, it's a Underwood No. 5, dates back to early 1900s. The man liked a classic! It has a value in its own right.'

Jules pondered this over the weekend while he got on with the usual mix of chores and recreation. He didn't tell either Jem or Archie about the typewriter, but he thought about it a lot. "What's got into you?" Jem grumbled at one point. "You're quiet."

"I'm thirty now," he archly reminded her. "This is the new improved mature Jules."

She sniffed. "Improved? The jury's still out on that, mate."

The thing was, the response to his email had added verisimilitude to the offer. The information provided wasn't exactly anything Jules didn't already know – but, then, how would he have judged the truth of something he'd been told 'out of the blue', as it were?

Eventually, on Monday around lunchtime, Jules replied with another question. 'If it's so old, does it still work? After all, apparently Ewan Byge was still writing his novels on it until recently.'

Within an hour or so came the response. 'It comes with the warning: Working machine, refurbished over the years. Collectible for fans of the writer, not anyone wanting a genuine original!'

Jules pondered some more while he sipped at a fresh coffee that was still a tad too hot.

Another email pinged in. 'We have an account with the clearing house. Can request a 10% discount and pass that on to buyer.'

Well. That made it rather more doable. Jules took another mouthful of coffee. 'Give me a final figure, including tax, and payment details, and I'll think about it.'

'£630 all inclusive. We use bank transfers for the large items.' The details followed, including sort code, account number and name, and even the IBAN. All with a reputable international bank, as well. So while Jules was aware there were fewer protections around direct bank transfers than there were with, say, credit card payments, this was more than offset by the fact he now had all these details – and the account itself wouldn't have even existed if the bank hadn't been convinced of the holder's bona fides.

He sighed. After another few minutes of thought, an idea occurred to him. Jules put down his coffee and headed upstairs to his bedroom, where he quickly found one of his autographed photos of Ewan Byge safely tucked away in a display folder. This photo had been personalised 'To Jules, with love'. Jules couldn't help but smile just seeing it again, and he let a careful fingerpad drift over the Sharpie ink. Then he took the photo over to his framed manuscript page, and he held it up close so he could compare the handwritten 'yare' to the message on the photo.

His initial instinct was that it was a match, but Jules made himself compare the letters. The only one in common was the 'e', so he examined every aspect of that. He was no handwriting expert, of course, but they looked plenty close enough, if you allowed for a different time and place, different circumstances, different pens. And the remaining letters were a good fit. The 'a' wasn't a stranger to the 'e', and the 'y' wasn't so different from the 'J'. And Jules knew that Ewan Byge Himself had written the message on the photo, because it had been at a book fair, and Jules had been Right There Swooning.

So Jules could conclude with a fair amount of comfort that the annotated manuscript page was genuine. Which meant that the typewriter must be, too. Not forgetting that he now had the guy's bank details.

'All right,' Jules finally replied to the email that afternoon, just before Archie was due home, 'I'll send you the money now. Let me know when I can expect the typewriter. Thank you!' And he couldn't help but add, 'I'm going to get a little excited now!'

Jules let that excitement get all pent up, and it bubbled away inside him – and he still didn't tell Archie or Jem, despite Jem narrowing her eyes at him a time or two, as if suspicious of who-knew-what mischief.

On the Wednesday, Jules ended up confessing all to his colleague Ryan while they were making mugs of what passed for coffee at the office. "So, anyway, I know it's *such* an extravagance …" Jules finally concluded.

Ryan nodded thoughtfully, and pondered through a moment's silence, but then he said, "That's the perfect piece of memorabilia, though, isn't it? I mean, seeing as you love the guy's writing so much."

"Yes," Jules gushed. "Yes, I thought so!"

"That's just awesome. Well done," Ryan added. And he nodded again, with what felt like respect.

Jules just beamed at him. Honestly, they were complete opposites – Ryan was straight and subtle and sensible – but they'd started at the accountancy on the same day, and provided each other whatever support was needed whether moral or im. Every Wednesday when they met at the office, they made a point of catching up with each other. Jules thought it was sweet. He assumed Ryan felt likewise, though of course he'd use a word such as 'cool'.

Ryan's support saw Jules through the rest of the week and into the weekend. The fact that Jules had already made a full confession also helped when Jem started poking and prodding. "What's got into you?" she asked. "You're hatching some scheme, aren't you?"

He tossed his head in as dignified a manner as he could manage. "And what if I am?"

"Come on, give. You know how bad you are at keeping a secret."

This was true, but Jules could feel a misgiving or two settling in his stomach. It was sheer cowardice, he knew, but he didn't want to tell Jem or Archie about the typewriter until he had the thing in all its meaning and glory. Jules tried a flank attack. "What if it's a surprise for you?" he asked – though it wasn't her birthday for three months, and Christmas was longer away yet. "What if it's a present?"

Jem took this seriously but also doubtfully. "Is it?"

"No."

Jem rolled her eyes. "Get it out of you sooner or later," she muttered, heading off and leaving him be.

Jules sighed. It was true he wouldn't hold out very long. He dragged his laptop over, and did a quick search to find the latest email exchange about his purchase. 'Hello! I am getting more than a little excited here. Do we have an ETA for delivery?'

A reply pinged in about half an hour later. 'Can you confirm your address for me?'

Jules did so – and then had to suffer through dinner while waiting for a further response.

Finally another email pinged in. 'Identified your payment. Took a while.'

Jules felt a modicum of annoyance at that, but it was obvious that this guy with his text-only emails and abruptness was not brilliant in the customer service department. Nor was he well organised. That should only help to make him come across as genuine, shouldn't it?

'Glad it arrived safely,' Jules replied. 'Sorry to ask again, but do we have an ETA for the typewriter?'

'These things can take a little time,' was the enigmatic response.

Jules shrugged, and gave up before he really did get annoyed. He didn't want to tarnish this self-indulgent treat of his. He powered down the laptop, and went to curl up on his bed with his Kindle instead. There were romances to be read, and therefore all was right with the world.

The doorbell rang that Tuesday, and Jules danced to the front door, absolutely sure that the typewriter must have finally arrived. "Hellooooo!" he warbled as he flung the door open wide.

"Hello, Mr Madigan," said the long-suffering Bart, handing over a padded envelope. "Regular mail, this is, but too big to put through the letterbox. Don't need to sign for it."

Jules took the thing, and propped it by the hallstand. Not only wasn't it typewriter-shaped, it was for Jem, so he really wasn't interested. The problem was that Bart was already turning away. "Wait a moment," Jules said. "Please. Isn't there a parcel for me?" He indicated the possible dimensions with his hands. "Probably a bit large and heavy. Maybe it's down the bottom of your van? I could come and fetch it …"

Bart had been shaking his head this whole time. "I would o' noticed something for you, Mr Madigan, and I wouldn't o' made you wait."

Well, Jules couldn't help but smile at that. "You *are* a sweetheart, Bart. Well, I guess I'll see you again soon, then!"

"Lookin' forward to it," Bart said in his usual stoic tones, as he finally turned and headed off down the steps. "See you, then."

"Thanks, Bart! See you!" Jules reluctantly stepped back inside and shut the door. The typewriter had to arrive soon. This was starting to become quite ridiculous.

"Been thinking," Jem announced over dinner a few evenings later.

Jules did his best *Aghast!* face, while Archie genially asked, "What about, love?"

"Been thinking, now that we're all three earning some decent money, we should look at buying a place. A house. A home."

Well. Whatever Jules had expected, it wasn't that. He gaped at her for a moment, before finding his voice. "Where did *that* come from?"

Jem shrugged. "Don't reckon we should be renting all our lives, should we? It's an investment."

"Is it? I mean, owning your own home. Not buying to rent; obviously that's an investment. But –"

"Owning our own place is investing in not having to pay rent when we're old. Just thinking about our future, yeah?"

She sounded very calm and sure about this. Jules gaped a bit more, and then turned to Archie, who'd remained quiet. "Dad? Is this something you've thought about?"

Archie looked mildly chagrined, which was pretty full-on for him. "I used to. I should have got us on the property ladder a long time ago. That first rung is a lot harder to reach these days."

"You weren't to know the economy would go so pear-shaped," Jem offered, while Jules made 'Don't worry about it' murmurs.

"I should have made more of an effort."

"You had the two of us to look after," Jules argued.

"Exactly," Archie said, looking at Jules directly with that honest gaze of his.

"No, I didn't mean –"

"I know, son." Archie patted Jules' hand reassuringly, before turning to Jem. "I'm not sure now, though, love. You two will each be wanting to set up your own households at some point. Make your own families."

"With you, too, though, Dad," Jules protested.

"I'm never settling down," Jem firmly added.

Archie smiled at Jules, though he spoke to Jem. "Jules will get married one day, and he should feel free to make his own decisions when he does. I don't want him tied down to me or a mortgage."

Jules clutched at Archie's hand, wondering why on earth Archie imagined Jules would ever choose a life that didn't involve his Dad.

"You'll want it to be just the two of you," Archie continued to Jules. "And then maybe there'll be kids …"

Jules kind of boggled at that. Even his imagination had rarely ventured past the honeymoon. "But – but – the kids will want their granddaddy! Of course! And even their wicked Auntie Jemima."

Archie smiled fondly.

Jem said, "Well, you guys are all the family I'll ever want or need. Along with Jules' husband and a brood of Mini Jules, I guess. So, tell me no if you don't want to do this, but as far as I'm concerned it makes sense."

"Wow," said Jules, somewhat in awe.

"Except for the Auntie bit. You tell your kids to call me that, and you are dead to me, Jules Madigan."

"Wow," he said again, rather more subdued.

"Wow, indeed," Archie agreed.

Jules sent another email about the typewriter. But this time, there was no reply.

"Been thinking some more," Jem said over another family dinner.

"Oh God, what now?" Jules muttered. Jem gave him a sardonic stare, while Archie glanced at him with gentle chastisement. "All right, all right. What have you been thinking about?"

"Happy here, aren't we? In this house? Maybe we should make an offer on it. If, you know, it still has plenty of leasehold."

Jules cast a doubting look about the place. It was a Victorian-era terrace house, a shabby little old lady, comfortable but nothing out of the ordinary. As with most of these places, there were two bedrooms on the top floor – those were his and Jem's. The ground floor was the living room at the front, then past the stairs to the room they were in now, set up with the kitchen table and chairs as well as Jules' work desk. Then the kitchen opened out of that, with the bathroom off to the left. Out the back was a narrow strip of land that was half ramshackle pavers and half weeds. Underneath the house was the basement 'flat', which was now Archie's room. He definitely had the most space to himself, though it was a bit dim and dingy down there, Jules had to admit. He asked, "Couldn't we manage anything better?"

Jem shrugged. "Probably not."

"What's the point, then?"

"So we're not forced to live somewhere even worse once we're old and grey."

Jules let out a huff. "Speak for yourself! I'm never going grey."

Another sardonic look was aimed his way. "Once we're old and dying our hair ginger."

Jules didn't bother replying. None of this was much fun … Not that it was supposed to be, he guessed. This was Real Life. Ho-bloody-hum!

Apparently Archie had been waiting on Jules to respond, but when he didn't, Archie said, "Whatever you two decide, I'll go along with. I'll be happy to help, if that's what you want to do."

"Thanks, Archie," said Jemima, with that cute little wrinkle of her nose she wielded infrequently but to excellent effect.

"Thanks, Dad," Jules echoed. But he didn't say anything further about the matter, and Jem didn't push.

"What's up with you, Ginger Spice?" Jem asked Jules a bit later. She was in her armchair and Jules was slouched on the sofa, and they were both giving half their attention to *The One Show*.

"Nothing," he insisted. Though he could hardly meet her gaze.

"Something's bothering you. Is it work, or something? They keep you busy – too busy. Strict deadlines doin' your head in?"

Jules shrugged. "No, it's fine."

Jem gave him her best sceptical look. But then after a moment she softened a little. "Is it … you know … the whole 'True Love' Problem, or lack thereof?"

He scowled at her. "No. That's not *all* I think about, you know!"

"Yeah, right." She slid her gaze away, obviously not willing to confront him too directly on such a sensitive matter.

"There's more to love than the romantic sort, anyway, isn't there?" he blundered on. "Remember how in *Maleficent*, the True Love Kiss was between the witch and her step-daughter? Foster-daughter. Whatever. And in *Frozen*, it was between the two sisters! I thought that was marvellous."

Jem was grinning at him with wry affection. "Oh, Jules, you're hopeless."

"Actually, I have it on good authority that I'm entirely loveable!" he archly responded.

"Yeah, well, you can just sod off, mate. *I'm* not gonna be kissing you."

"No, 'cause I can run faster!"

"Cannot."

"Can, too."

"Children!" cried Archie as he came into the living room. "Enough. Oh, what wouldn't I give for a little peace and quiet?"

"Sorry, Dad," said Jules.

Jemima poked her tongue out at him behind Archie's back.

"So, how's the typewriter?" Ryan asked, two Wednesdays later. "It must be a thrill!" He swept enthusiastically on, apparently not registering Jules' glum face. "I was just thinking the other day, how awesome it must be to touch the keys, and think that's exactly where the author's fingers were when he was writing your favourite novel."

Jules sighed. He wasn't even up for a big dramatic sigh, but only a sad little exhalation.

Ryan finally noticed. "Oh. What's up?"

"It hasn't arrived yet."

"But it should have, right? I mean, what was the delivery date?"

"Well ..." Jules squirmed a bit. "He never quite said. I asked for an ETA – a few times – and he just kind of never quite answered."

"Oh." Ryan considered him with a gaze turned cool.

"I'm sure it'll turn up!" Jules brightly declared.

"Oh, sure, yeah," Ryan agreed. "These things can take time."

"That's just what the guy I'm buying it from said!"

"Proper packing, and ... and, like, making sure it has the proper provenance and all."

"Of course." Jules nodded, probably overdoing it a bit. Ryan lifted his coffee mug in a silent toast to him, and headed back to the hot desks. Jules trailed after him.

The coffee in Jules' own mug was steaming reassuringly, but Jules felt sour, and he didn't think he could stomach it.

'I'm getting a tad nervous now,' Jules sent via email. 'You understand. I parted with a tidy sum of money, and have nothing to show for it yet. Can you please send something – anything – a scan of the order or even the original listing from the clearing house? Just to put my little mind at rest.'

Silence.

He opened up eBay, and browsed to find the guy's shop page. Even though it looked quiet with no new items available, it was all still there, and the guy had a feedback rating in the nineties. The listings were all things such as autographs, scripts and manuscript pages, however, rather than the more solid memorabilia offered via email.

Jules clicked on the Help & Contact link, and browsed the eBay policies. Within moments he was reading, 'We don't allow our members to use eBay to contact each other to make offers to buy or sell items outside of eBay.' Jules sighed. He'd known all along it wasn't strictly legit, hadn't he?

A month to the day after Jules had made the bank transfer, he sat over dinner, quiet and full of dread. He'd made his favourite as consolation – lemon chicken risotto – but could hardly eat a mouthful. Archie watched him in concern, while Jem maintained a tart 'I knew it!' expression.

Finally Jules said, "I've got something to tell you both."

Archie reached to pat Jules' hand reassuringly, while Jem just said, "At last."

"Jemima," Archie chided.

Jules took a long moment, but it wasn't going to get any easier. "I've been an idiot," he announced.

"Go on, son. There's very few things in life that can't be undone."

"This might be one of them." Jules sighed, and then finally confessed. "That manuscript page I bought. The last page of the last book that Ewan Byge wrote on his old typewriter? Well, the typewriter itself became available. And – I bought it."

"What?!" Jemima cried. "You spend over a hundred quid on a bit of paper – and then what? You're just throwing your money away these days, are you?"

He was curled up so far that his face was almost in his dinner. Jules lifted up far enough to shoot a grimace at her. "This all happened before I knew you had these real estate dreams."

"I don't even want to know how much you've wasted on this." She scowled at him, hard. "No, tell me. How much? We're never even gonna get a deposit together at this rate!"

Jules gazed miserably into his lukewarm risotto, and thought he may never cook that again.

Archie reached a supportive hand to grasp Jules's shoulder. "Is it a joy to you, son? This typewriter. One of the old classics, from what you've said before. If it's true what they say about a thing of beauty being a joy forever, then I'm sure it was worth it."

"Hah!"

"Now, Jemima, we're all allowed our foibles."

"Not so little, this one, for sure."

Archie turned back to Jules. "Can we see it? Is it in your room?"

Jules finally sat up straight with his spine against the wooden back of the chair, and he faced the music. "It hasn't arrived. I think – it's been a month now. I mean, I know it's been a month now, since I ordered it. And it hasn't arrived."

Silence.

"So the thing is … I think I've been scammed."

"Oh, you stupid bloody idiot, Jules."

"Jemima!" Archie protested.

"Yes, all right, all right," she bitterly replied. She stood, and grabbed up her bag and keys. "Going out. Bloody stupid thing to do, Jules."

"I know," he admitted.

"So, get this fucking thing sorted, then."

And with a clattering of heels and a slamming of doors, she was gone.

Archie had instinctively turned towards the front door, with a 'Stay safe!' on his lips. But he and Jules were long used to Jem's insistence on coming and going as she pleased, and not being asked for particulars. Archie turned back to the table and their interrupted dinner.

Jules fell into the nearest hug available. Which was his Dad's, of course. Always and forever his Dad's.

Jules went to fetch his laptop. He and Archie opened up Google and typed 'I think I've been defrauded'. The first result took them to the police's Action Fraud site. "'Sometimes people choose not to report fraud because they are embarrassed that they fell for a scam'," Jules read out loud. "Yeah," he agreed with a sigh. "I *have* been an idiot. Jem was right."

"Jemima was being very hard on you," Archie replied.

"And so she should be."

"She'll calm down. She'll forgive you." Archie put an arm around Jules' shoulders, and squeezed. "You'll forgive yourself."

He couldn't see that happening, or not any time soon, so instead Jules read through the page of advice on the website. If he wanted to go ahead and report the matter, there was an online form he could complete, or a phone number to call. Well, that was a no-brainer of a choice. He clicked open the form.

Jules and Archie started working through the questions, but on a certain page they got stuck. All they had to go on at this point was that the typewriter hadn't arrived, and the Bad Guy wasn't returning emails. Apparently that wasn't in itself enough to make a case.

Jules sighed and sat back. "So there's nothing we can do? That doesn't seem right."

"Can't eBay help? Surely they have some kind of fraud protection program."

"But I didn't buy it through eBay. Not the typewriter. Yes, there's protections if you do, but I bought this from a follow-up email." Jules admitted, "I should have known better."

"Oh," said Archie, temporarily stymied. "Then, how about the bank? Maybe they can help. Credit card purchases are protected, aren't they?"

Jules knew all about that, unfortunately. "He asked for a bank transfer. There aren't any protections around that. I even thought about that at the time, but I figured if he has a proper bank account with a proper bank then at least we know who he is."

Archie stared at him with more sympathy and sorrow than disapproval. But after a while, he asked what Jem hadn't: "How much are we talking about, son?"

Jules steeled himself. "Six hundred and thirty pounds."

Despite himself, a wince twisted Archie's face.

"That's not even a month's mortgage payment!"

"All the more reason why we'd need it, son, if we go ahead with Jem's plans."

Jules flared into resentment. "What does she want to tie us down like that for? If we'd bought a place back home, we could never have moved to London. Why can't we just have fun, and be free to live where we want?"

"Be free to be destitute in our old age?"

"It won't come to that. Anyway," Jules said, lifting his gaze to Archie's, "you know we'll look after you, no matter what."

"Thank you, Jules – but I'm more worried about the two of you. Jemima, especially, if she's never going to settle down with a partner. These days, you plan ahead on the basis that you'll need to take care of yourselves."

Jules rolled back his shoulders in an ambivalent shrug. Maybe, as an accountant, he was meant to be more serious than this, but he was far more interested in the present than the past or the future, and he never planned more than a week ahead if he could help it.

"You should come into work with me one day," Archie continued. "There's some lessons to be learnt there."

Well, that sounded like fun. Not.

But Archie's eyes had a sudden twinkle in them.

"What's going on with you at work?" Jules asked suspiciously.

Archie just stood and started collecting the dinner plates. "Let's get this washed up," he said. "There's a program I want to watch at nine."

Four

"For God's sake, you're an accountant now!" Jem burst out when she finally came home the next evening.

"Um, yes," Jules agreed, not really sure where that came from.

"Thought you'd finally get serious. Quit frittering away your life."

Well, he'd known she thought along those lines, but that still stung. "Frittering away?"

"All this 'Big Romantic Stuff', like the man said."

"It was a *typewriter*."

"Exactly. We should be thinking about investments, not indulgences."

"Okay, okay, I get that, I *do*. But it's like you've already made the decision – for all of us. Give me a chance to catch up, all right?"

She softened a little, and after a long moment she acknowledged, "All right, fair point."

"It was just a bit out of the blue, Jem."

"Okay, I get that, too." Jem nodded thoughtfully, and turned to head upstairs. At the doorway, she said, "Let me know if you get on board, yeah?"

"When I get on board, sure."

She left with an agreeable sounding huff of breath. Which made Jules all the more determined to do what he could to get his money back if it was at all possible.

It occurred to Jules that if he wanted to report this as fraud, then he'd have to do some legwork himself. Some detective work, even. It was up to him now. If it was no use simply saying that the typewriter had never turned up, then he'd have to find some extra proof or evidence that he'd been had.

After a day or so of pondering, he figured he might as well try going direct to the source. Or to the source's agent, anyway. The link to Ewan Byge's page on his agent's website was, of course, saved in Jules' Favourites. He called up the page, thought for a moment, then clicked on the email address link for the agent, Maryann Bryant, rather than the assistant. A new message window popped up.

'Query re possible fraud', Jules typed into the subject line. That should get someone's attention.

'Dear Maryann,' he began. 'Following an eBay transaction, I was contacted via email by the seller. I was offered for sale Ewan Byge's old Underwood No. 5 manual typewriter (available since his publisher gave him a laptop). As a fan of Ewan, I sent the seller a fair amount of money a month ago, but the typewriter has never been delivered. At this point, I suspect I have been defrauded.

'Can you please confirm whether the typewriter has been made available for sale at any time, and if so via whom?

'Yours in mingled hope and chagrin, Jules Madigan.'

Jules considered this for a while, and re-read it twice. He changed 'As a fan of Ewan' to refer to 'Ewan's novels' instead of the man himself. And then he hit the Send button.

When Jules logged in the next morning, he was astonished to find a message from the agent already waiting in his Inbox. He'd hardly dared to hope they'd reply, let alone so promptly. Jules took a moment to reflect that this situation must really matter to them … unlike many fannish requests.

'Dear Mr Madigan,

'I'm very sorry to say that it seems we have bad news. We know where the typewriter in question is – in fact, we know where both of them are, for Mr Byge used two alternately – and they are definitely not available for sale. I'm afraid it seems that you have been misled.

'If you would be prepared to share with me the seller's name, whether the company or the individual or both, I will be able to confirm whether this is someone with whom we do business.

'I apologise again for being the bearer of bad tidings.'

After a month of increasing worry, it was frankly a relief to know for sure where he stood. Jules felt oddly light-hearted. He hit the Reply button.

'Thank you very much for your quick response. The seller's name is –'

Jules felt a qualm, and stopped with his fingers hovering over the keyboard. He had been careful not to make a direct accusation before now. He hadn't said anything unreasonable let alone libellous. Even if this question and answer were in the honest spirit of inquiry, a cunning lawyer could probably make a good deal out of it.

Jules sighed and typed the name. He continued, 'The seller mentioned a clearing house through which he was sourcing the memorabilia. Whether that exists or not, I never saw it named.'

The response came back within an hour. 'I can confirm that this individual is not someone we have done business with directly, and such transactions would not be handled through any organisation that could reasonably be called a clearing house. Again, apologies for the bad news. Mr Byge asked me to pass on his warm concern about the situation in which you find yourself.'

Mr Byge! Oh My God! Ewan Byge was passing on his 'warm concern' to Jules Madigan! Jules' heart leapt and started skipping pitterty-pat, pitterty-pat. That must mean that Ewan Byge had heard Jules' name, and the story, and despite Jules being such an idiot, Ewan still sent his warm concern … Oh my oh my oh my.

Jules was all aflutter now. What price that?

Well, 'what price' was actually six hundred and thirty pounds, Jules reflected some while later.

Still, never mind that. He felt as if he was standing on solid ground again.

This time when he filled out the Action Fraud online form, the extra information he could provide was enough for him to complete and submit the thing. He was automatically assigned a reference number, and he could now sit back and leave it all in the hands of the City of London Police.

Jem worked out how much dosh they needed as a deposit to buy a house similar to the one they were renting. It was a scary figure. So scary that, to be honest, Jules didn't feel that six hundred and thirty pounds made all that much difference one way or another. Still, he had to try to do his bit. He was rather embarrassed to find that Jem had been regularly saving something out of her salary each month, which had already mounted up to a tidy sum. Archie was willing to contribute a good proportion of his lump sum from when he retired, even though that would reduce his future income. Jules, in contrast, had pretty much wiped out his current account with the purchase of the typewriter, and had spent most of August trying not to dip into credit.

They'd all learned frugal ways, however, back in the days when they'd had no other choice, so it wasn't as if they couldn't be careful now, despite living in one of the more expensive cities in the world.

"I've done the sums," Jem announced, "and reckon we could pull together a deposit within a couple of years, if we try."

Archie nodded, but looked at Jules. "I'm not sure you're entirely convinced, son. There's no point in starting this unless we mean to all commit to it."

"I guess …" Jules looked around them at the ramshackle house in question. "I guess we'd only be able to afford a place something like this, right?"

"Probably," Jem agreed.

"If we buy it, though, all the problems become our problems, don't they? Not the landlord's."

Jem sagged a little. "Fair point. What d'you see us doing instead, though? Renting places that are borderline, and once they're unbearable, moving on to another place that seems marginally better – until it falls apart, too?"

"If it's going to fall apart, why would we want to *own* it? Doesn't sound like much of an investment in our future, and all that."

"Okay," said Jem. "I get it." Apparently Jules had managed to take the wind out of her sails. "Okay. Let me think about that, all right?"

"All right," he agreed. But Jules figured that whatever she decided to do now, he'd go along with.

Jules received another automatically generated email from Action Fraud, advising that his case had been assigned to Police Constable Leonard Edgar. Within half an hour, an email popped in from PC Edgar himself.

'Good afternoon, Mr Madigan.

'Thank you for taking the time to submit your report to Action Fraud. I look forward to working on this case.

'Could you please forward any emails and other evidence regarding this transaction to me at this address, including a screen capture or scan of the bank statement which details the payment you made? Once I have reviewed them, I will make an appointment to meet with you and take your witness statement.

'Should you have any queries or concerns, please do not hesitate to contact me via email. Alternatively, call the City of London number in the footer, quoting my badge number.

'Thank you again for your efforts.

'Best regards, Leonard Edgar'

Jules sat back and for a moment indulged himself by rubbing his hands together in glee. It seemed it wasn't all such a lost cause after all. At least Jules could feel as if he were doing something useful.

He copied PC Edgar's email address, and then searched for the first email he'd received from the Bad Guy.

After another exchange of emails, Jules agreed that PC Edgar would meet him after work that Wednesday, so that Jules could give his statement. Ryan happened to walk out of the office with Jules, so the two of them were shoulder to shoulder when they saw the uniformed police officer waiting on the pavement. PC Edgar's gaze, however, latched onto Jules immediately – and Jules wasn't overly surprised, as the officer must have researched Jules as well as the Bad Guy over the past few days, and there were plenty of photos of Jules on Facebook and Twitter. It didn't take great detective skills for him to then pick out the pasty-skinned Carrot Top from the line-up.

"Good evening, Mr Madigan," said PC Edgar, stepping forward with his hand out to shake.

Jules shook the hand – lean and strong – and said with very little aplomb, "Oh, hi, uh … do I call you Constable Edgar?"

"Yes, but just Leonard would be fine, if you like." The man had a pleasant enough face, or at least a pleasant expression, but his gaze was so fixed upon Jules that it was unsettling.

Ryan said, "Do you have your credentials?"

At last that gaze snapped away for a moment. "Oh, of course." The police officer produced a wallet after only a brief fumble, and displayed his badge and warrant card to Jules first and then to Ryan. "I apologise. I should have had it ready."

"That's all right," Jules said, widening his eyes at Ryan in a query. "I mean, the uniform makes it pretty obvious who you are." There were more doodads and details to the officer's clothes and accessories than Jules could imagine anyone but a genuine cop bothering with. Apart from which,

Constable Edgar had known Jules' name, and known to meet him here. Who else could he be?

"Just wanted to be sure," Ryan stoutly replied.

"Of course," Constable Edgar agreed, with no hint at all that he minded being doubted. "If you want to accompany Mr Madigan, sir, that would be perfectly acceptable. I thought we could go to the nearest police station, Mr Madigan, but I can take your statement anywhere that's comfortable for you."

"Jules?" Ryan asked. "D'you want me to come along?"

"No, that's fine. That's really not necessary." It hadn't even occurred to Jules that he needed company for this. And it wasn't that he didn't trust the Constable, even though the guy made him feel a bit edgy with his stare. He was probably just wondering how anyone reached thirty years old and a professional job when they were so gullible and naïve. Well, it was obviously time for Jules to start standing a little firmer on his own two feet, and be seen to do so. "I'll be fine, Ryan," he said.

"All right." Ryan cast another look over both the Constable and Jules as he began walking away. "Text me later, Jules. All right?"

"Yes, okay," Jules replied, though it was completely unnecessary. When Ryan looked back again, Jules saw him off with a wave and a warm smile. Then Jules turned in beside Constable Edgar, and they began walking in the direction of the police station on Maitland Street.

"I've booked an interview room," Constable Edgar said, "but we can do this anywhere you like. At a café, for example. I could buy you a coffee. Or a tea."

"That's fine," said Jules.

Edgar glanced at him. "Being at the station does make the process more straightforward. I can type up the statement in the proper format, and you can read and sign it right away. If I just take notes, then I have to type it up later, and meet you again for you to check it …"

"Honestly, I'm happy to come to the station."

"Your … friend was concerned."

Jules turned his head away so he could roll his eyes. Talk about mountains and molehills. "I really don't know where that came from. I didn't ask him to walk out with me to meet you tonight."

The Constable smiled. "It's good to have a … friend who cares for you."

Jules indulged in another eye-roll, though in self-mockery this time. Of course it would have been quickly obvious to anyone Googling Jules that he was gay, gay, gay. "Ryan's not my boyfriend, if that's what you're asking. He's straight, for a start. And a colleague. We started at the accountancy on the same day, so I guess we just buddied up."

"That's very good indeed," the Constable replied, his smile only broadening – though never quite parting his lips.

"Yes, it is," Jules muttered. And that seemed to do the trick, as they walked on in silence.

The interview room was very basic and rather shabby. An absolutely minimal amount of old furniture, a desktop PC from the Stone Age, and painted walls that had done at least twenty years hard labour. Jules looked around and huffed a laugh. "Not as high-tech as on the telly, then."

Edgar huffed, too. "That's the fantasy. Welcome to the reality, Mr Madigan!"

"*Please* just call me Jules," he asked as he sat in the visitor's chair.

"If you'll call me Leonard," was the response. The Constable raised an eyebrow and considered Jules with the tiniest hint of a challenge.

"Yes, all right. Leonard."

"Thank you, Jules," he replied with a pleased look. Leonard sat down in the other chair, across the desk from Jules, and logged into the computer. The keyboard was in front of him, but the screen was set off to the far side, angled towards Leonard but not so far that they couldn't both see it. "I'll just call up the statement form and fill in the details. Won't be long," he added with a friendly glance.

"Not a problem," Jules said. He looked around the room again, but there was nothing even remotely as interesting as Police Constable Leonard Edgar, so Jules turned a considering gaze on him. It wasn't as if Leonard hadn't been watching Jules this whole time. In any case, Leonard seemed completely unselfconscious, as if it was nothing to him whether he was watched or not.

Jules thought the other man must be somewhat older than him, perhaps as much as forty. He had very dark hair, almost black, but it seemed to be silvering a little at the temples. He was lean, but in a strong and wiry way, and his skin was a lovely olive colour, as if he made the most of London's limited sunshine. Leonard's face was likewise weathered and lean, which perhaps made him seem older than he really was, but the bright dark eyes either side of a large sharp blade of a nose made him seem younger again, or at least young in mind. This was obviously a man who was intelligent, and fit, and spent time outdoors. Perhaps he even ran marathons and such – he had a runner's hard body. All pretty much the complete opposite of pale pudgy Jules!

A sigh snapped that clear dark glance back to Jules again. "Almost there," Leonard said, tapping away at the keys like a professional ten-fingered touch typist.

"That's fine." Jules had warned Archie and Jem that he'd be late, and dinner was basically going to be reheated lasagne from the previous night with a fresh salad, so he really wasn't in a hurry.

"Right," said Leonard after another moment. "You're a fan of this author, Ewan –"

"Ewan Byge," Jules gushed, "spelt B-Y-G-E, pronounced 'bi'."

Leonard stopped typing, and just looked at him. It would have taken a career-hardened criminal not to break under that regard.

"He writes the most fabulous romances. I mean, they're fantastic, they just sweep you away – and they're real, too. He means every word! He was a huge part of the Marriage Equality campaign, so you know when he writes about True Love and Happy Ever After, he feels it, too – body, heart and soul."

"True love," Leonard said, in pondering tones. He called something up on the computer, which proved to be one of the emails Jules had sent him. "*The 'True Love' Solution*. You bought a page of the manuscript for that novel."

"Yes. It was the last thing Ewan actually wrote on the typewriter, you see."

Leonard paused for a moment, and then asked in scrupulously neutral tones, "Was the page genuine or fake?"

Jules grimaced. Obviously he'd thought long and hard about that, but he had to admit, "I don't know. It seems genuine. It's not just a photocopy; you can feel the indentations from the keys. And there's an edit on it in blue ink that looks like Ewan's handwriting. But it wouldn't be hard to fake it.

Probably even I could manage something pretty convincing."

"But your Action Fraud report is just about the typewriter."

"Yes. Well. I still have the page hanging on my bedroom wall. Framed. I like to believe it's the real thing. Of course I've wondered about it, a lot, since the typewriter failed to show ..." Jules sagged into a frown. "I suppose I'm just not prepared to make an accusation I'm not sure of."

Leonard nodded. "I'll probably ask the agent, Ms Bryant, as part of my investigation. If you want to know?"

Did he want that taken away from him as well? Jules let out a sigh.

"What I'm thinking," Leonard offered, with a tentative note Jules hadn't heard from him before, "is that Ewan Byge is concerned about the situation."

Jules sat up again, and beamed. "He is, that's true!"

"So, if the page you have turns out to be a fake, I'm sure he'd be willing to provide a genuine replacement or substitute. If you don't want to ask Ms Bryant, I'll suggest it myself."

"Oh, that's brilliant! What a terrific idea!"

Leonard lowered his gaze and apparently tried to repress a grin. He was only marginally successful. "Well, it would be good if you got something out of this. I'm afraid," Leonard continued, looking directly at Jules again, "there isn't much chance of you getting your money back. Even if this matter comes to court and he's found guilty, I can't promise that it will result in compensation for the victims."

"No, well." Jules sighed. "That's okay. It's the right thing to do anyway, isn't it? He shouldn't be allowed to get away with taking advantage of fans, you know? That's just not fair."

"Agreed." Leonard lined up his hands on the keyboard and alt-tabbed to another email. "Right. So this started on the twenty-ninth of June when you successfully bid for a manuscript page on eBay. Is that correct, Mr Madigan?"

"Yes, Constable Edgar," Jules replied with only the mildest facetiousness.

An amused flash of those sharp dark eyes, and Leonard started typing out the statement, translating aloud into the City of London Police dialect as he went.

Jules had assumed he'd just catch the Tube home as usual, but Leonard insisted on signing out a police car and driving him home. Apparently it was The Done Thing. Which was kind of cool. Jules was expected to sit in the back seat, but the two of them nattered away about the relative merits of the suburbs in which they each lived. Or, to be more accurate, the suburbs in which Leonard had previously lived, because apparently he was now living at the City of London Police section house.

"Oh," said Jules. "I didn't even know you could do that."

"It's just single rooms and shared facilities. More like student housing than a hotel. Certainly nothing like an apartment block."

"So, is that ... fun, or not so much?"

Leonard cast him a glance via the rear-view mirror, and admitted, "Not so much. It can be bedlam, and of course the section house is where they come looking when a beat officer is unavailable, or they need more uniforms for a serious incident. But it's relatively cheap, and convenient, and –" Leonard paused, and then seemed to halt entirely, as if feeling he'd already said too much.

"I'm sure it's very convenient," Jules said, "and it must make it easier to be living with people who understand the nature of your work. I mean, if you work a late shift, or you have a particularly difficult day, then you're with people who know exactly what that's like."

"Yes, you're right," said Leonard, not entirely convincingly. "Though I have to say it wouldn't be my first choice, if I had any family left living in London."

"Of course," Jules agreed in easy tones, sensing that Leonard wouldn't appreciate excessive sympathy.

Jules had spent much of the journey watching the streets and the passing traffic and pedestrians, and wondering if anyone seeing him in the back seat of a cop car would assume he was a criminal. Once upon a time that might have bothered him, but now he just shrugged off the idea with barely a second thought.

"I'll be in touch, Mr Madigan," Leonard said, once they were outside the terrace house. He'd come around to open the door for his passenger. "Jules. I'll let you know how the case progresses."

"Fantastic," Jules replied. "Have fun with the investigation!"

Leonard grinned a bit wolfishly. "Thank you. I'll call you soon."

Five

Leonard didn't call – but to Jules' surprise, Leonard was waiting outside the accountancy office for Jules on the following Wednesday after work. "Good evening, Mr Madigan," he said, standing there at the bottom of the steps, just exactly where he'd stood the previous week. There was a small smile on his face, and he was in regular clothes.

"Hello! I wasn't expecting to see you!" Jules jogged down to the pavement, and grinned at the man. He only had to tilt his head back a fraction. "Did you have a break-through, or something? Are you on duty, or … ?"

"Or," replied Leonard. "I can give you an update on the case, certainly. But I had a couple of questions for you, as well, and I thought we might do that over coffee."

"Sounds good."

"Unless you need to get home?"

"Home can wait for half an hour. I'll probably get there quicker, anyway, if I'm not in the thick of rush hour."

Leonard allowed himself a proper smile for once. "Then, do you have a favourite café around here?"

"Sure!" And Jules led Leonard two blocks down and one across to Mr Oakley's Coffee House. "They're very particular about their coffee at Mr Oakley's. And they don't close at five-thirty like all the chains around here. Honestly, the City doesn't die the moment the working day is ended!"

"True," said Leonard as he held the door of Mr Oakley's open for Jules – who took the opportunity to cast an admiring glance at the man, because he was looking quite fine in his jeans and shirt and knitted jumper. Leonard grinned and dropped his head as if bashful.

"So how do you take it?" Jules asked as he slid into one of the booths. "Your coffee, I mean," he added after a perfectly timed pause.

"Milk and sugar," Leonard confessed as he sat opposite. "The section house coffee needs all the help it can get."

"Sounds like what they provide at the office. Mmm … I think I'm in the mood for a latte this evening."

A waiter came over to take their order – Daniel. Jules was on a first-name basis with all of them. Daniel winked at Jules for being there with a new companion, and acknowledged their requests with a little kick to his smile.

Once Daniel had gone again, Jules chuckled and said, "They probably all think this is a date, not an interrogation."

Leonard looked as if he was trying not to make an inappropriate retort. He settled for a very sober, "Just a follow-up interview, Mr Madigan."

"Fire away, then."

A moment passed. Leonard's natural position seemed to be with his head down as if concentrating on listening and thinking. Which all added to his considered, deliberate manner. Eventually he started, "May I ask …"

Another pause ensued while Daniel delivered their coffees, and Leonard added sugar to his.

And then, finally: "May I ask why you waited over a month before reporting the fraud?"

"Oh. Oh, well … I wasn't sure. And I didn't want to make any false accusations. And I kept coming up with ideas about what could have gone wrong. I kept hoping."

"Most people would have been more …"

"Sceptical?"

"Impatient."

Jules let out a sigh. "I guess … I wanted to believe. You know?"

Leonard nodded. "It seems like the classic fraud case to me. The initial sale of a smaller item, the offer of a discount, stringing you along."

"I've been horribly gullible, haven't I?"

"No," Leonard immediately protested. "Oh, no. You're very trusting." That small secret smile tilted his lips. "It's actually rather refreshing."

"Well, I'm glad you think so! I think Jem's going to kill me! Jemima," he added.

Leonard went still, and asked in an overly casual tone, "Who's Jemima?"

"My – well, my foster-sister, if you're taking notes. She was my best friend in school, and when her folks kind of imploded, back in Year 8, she came to live with me and my Dad. Haven't managed to get rid of her since."

"That was good of you."

"It was good of my Dad. Archie. He's the absolute best!"

"I'm sure he is."

"So, me and Jem, we're still best friends, but we've also got that whole 'edgy sibling' thing going on. Not the rivalry thing, but just making each other crazy on a regular basis. She wasn't exactly impressed at me throwing my money away like this. I mean, even if I *did* have the typewriter to show for it, she wouldn't have been impressed."

Leonard nodded thoughtfully, took a mouthful of coffee, and remained silent.

"But that's kind of off-topic. Do you have more questions?"

"Not really," Leonard admitted.

"How's the case going? You said you could give me an update?"

"Oh." Leonard sat up a little straighter, and drank some more as if to create a pause. "This is good," he remarked, indicating the coffee.

"It is, isn't it? I don't think they sell doughnuts here, that's the only problem."

Leonard cast him a sardonic glance, then said, "The case is going well. And I'm pleased to say that it will remain mine, as it comes under the City of London jurisdiction."

"Oh, that's good … But I got the impression from the website that all fraud was reported to London?"

"Reported, yes. When we identify the suspect, the case is transferred to the relevant police force."

"Ah! So you've definitely identified him, then?"

Leonard tilted his head slightly, as if considering. "You'll understand that I can't tell you the details, but I've made contact with the bank, with Mr Byge's agent, and with eBay. I don't know if you've seen, but his page has recently been closed down by eBay due to apparent infractions."

"So you might actually be able to arrest the Bad Guy?"

"I'm quietly confident." Leonard hardly seemed aware that he lay one hand on the wooden table top when he did that. They were both quiet for a moment in which they noticed that they'd finished their coffees. A decision needed to be made, about whether to order another drink or say goodnight. Leonard apparently went with the latter. "I mustn't take up any more of your evening, Jules. You have family waiting for you. I'll walk you to your Tube station."

"Oh, that's not necessary," Jules said, standing from the booth. "Neither's that," he added as Leonard went to pay.

"Nonsense. I invited you."

Daniel called goodnight to Jules, and winked again with a lift of his chin to indicate approval. Jules grinned at the guy and shook his head. Honestly, Jules was pretty sure Leonard was gay or bi or whatever, but it wasn't like this had actually been a date ... Which didn't, of course, stop Leonard from opening the coffee shop door for Jules, and then accompanying him all the way to the ticket barriers at the Tube station.

"Goodnight, Mr Madigan," said Leonard, somehow making this sound as warm and personal as any farewell could be.

"Goodnight, Constable Edgar," Jules replied, trying to do likewise. And with a smile he already knew was a tad fond, Jules turned away and touched his Oyster card to the card reader. The gates swept back to let him through.

Jem wasn't talking to Jules right now, or maybe she was just preoccupied. She'd been working extra shifts at the hotel, and Jules wasn't quite game enough to ask whether that was just because she had to or because she was trying to save up extra money. But Jules made them a Cajun soup that night, with spicy sausage, some leftover chicken, and corn, onions and tomatoes – and that at least provoked a smile from her.

"Well done, son," Archie said, even though the flavourings had made his eyes water, just a little.

"Yeah," drawled Jem. "You're a taste sensation, Ginger Jules."

"Takes one to know one, Juniper Jem."

"Ha!" she cried, sounding pleased. But she stood from the table, and gathered her phone and stuff. "I'm on early shift tomorrow, so I'll say goodnight, guys."

"Goodnight, Jemima," said Archie as she leant down to press a kiss to his cheek. "You take care of yourself, love."

"I will. Sleep tight, Archie!"

"Sleep tight," the two men chorused in response. And she disappeared up the stairs.

On the following Wednesday, Jules was half-expecting Leonard to meet him after work for another coffee. So around four p.m. when Grace the receptionist phoned his hot desk to announce a visitor, Jules just said, "Oh, sure. I'll be right down."

When he reached the ground floor, he found that the guest had been shown into the meeting room already rather than being made to wait in the foyer. There was more than one visitor, too, and his boss Bethany was there for some reason, talking in a low serious tone. Jules felt a qualm or two, but as soon as he turned the corner, the first thing he saw was exactly who he expected. "Hello, Leonard, or should I say Constable Edgar under the circumstances, I hope everything's o- ... oh my God, I mean my good golly gosh, Ewan Byge as I live and breathe."

For it was Ewan Byge Himself sitting at the meeting table – or standing now, with an amused grin on his face, standing and leaning forward to hold out his hand to shake, and saying, "You must be Jules Madigan."

"Oh my word, yes, that's me, yes, oh my."

Those glorious sea-green eyes narrowed a little. "I remember you. We've met before, haven't we?"

"At a book fair, yes, and a convention, or two – or three."

"Of course."

"It's the red hair," Jules explained, flipping a dismissive hand towards the hair in question, which that day thank heavens was dishevelled in only the most stylish of ways. Fie on his pale skin, though, which meant he could never hide a blush!

Ewan leaned forward a little again to say, "It's not just the hair. Is it, Leonard?" he added, jocularly elbowing the police officer in the ribs.

Luckily, Leonard was in his full uniform complete with padded vest so there'd be no bruising. However, he didn't seem to have a response to this assault other than blinking once and then freezing.

"Right," said Bethany, sitting down again, apparently hoping to put this back on a more business-like footing.

The three men all sat down, too. Jules hadn't thought to move, so he was kind of stuck on his own down one end of the table. He cast a sympathetic glance at Leonard, who seemed a bit pale beneath his olive skin, and he received a small friendly nod in response. But then Jules dared to look again at Ewan – who was looking at Bethany quite seriously, as if this were an actual business meeting. Which apparently it was.

"I've been looking for a proper accountant," Ewan began explaining.

"Well, when I say looking, I mean it's been on my To Do List. My brother-in-law, my sister's husband, has been doing my tax returns, every quarter and every year – but that's on top of his regular work, of course, and with their first baby on the way, I really shouldn't burden him any longer. And then my agent happened to mention that this one –" Ewan tipped his head towards Jules in a charmingly indulgent manner – "is an accountant, so when I was talking with Leonard, I asked him, and he said he didn't see the harm in me coming here and offering myself to you –" the briefest pause – "as a client."

Bethany looked as if her head was spinning from trying to follow all of that. "I see. Or, rather, I don't see entirely. But you're looking to engage our services, Mr –"

"Byge," Ewan and Jules choroused.

"B-Y-G-E, pronounced 'by'," Jules added.

Ewan winked at him. "That's very good. I'll have to use that."

Bethany was somehow managing to hang in there. "Mr Byge. You're wanting to engage our firm's services, and you're asking that Jules be your dedicated accountant?"

Ewan took a breath and said very solemnly, "I feel that I owe him a rather large favour."

Bethany took a breath in her turn, and glanced from Jules to Leonard and back to Ewan. "Heavens! I don't think I want to know the details."

Leonard cleared his throat. "There's been nothing untoward on Mr Madigan's part, Ms Tines." After a moment, he thought to add, "Nor on Mr Byge's part."

Which was a rather unfortunate phrase to use, but Jules managed not to giggle, and forced himself not to make eye contact with Ewan, who he suspected would have joined in the mirth.

"And you're a writer, Mr Byge? A novelist? I have to say that Jules' work mainly relates to IT and management consultants –"

"But how different could it be?" Jules pleaded. "It's not like he's an actor or anything. Your business is probably set up as a corporation," he continued to Ewan, "and VAT registered, seeing as you said quarterly returns. Is that right?"

"Yes, absolutely right." Though Ewan grimaced a grin, and added, "At least, as far as I understand it. I'm sure Ted would be happy to fill you in on all the details. My brother-in-law Ted."

"Perfect." Jules turned to Bethany, not ashamed to beg. "Please?"

Bethany rolled her eyes. "I'm not turning away a new client, Mr Byge – and I'm sure Jules can be your main point of contact at our office – but you'll understand that if I change my mind about that last point, it will be in your interests?"

Ewan nodded, and reached across to shake her hand. "Thank you, Bethany. And I'm sure you won't need to be changing your mind."

Jules came *this* close to swooning.

He might have just floated home that evening for all the notice he took of the mundane world. Ewan Byge had remembered him. Ewan Byge wanted to do him a favour. Ewan Byge would be his client, which meant they'd actually be in touch at least once every three months and maybe even more!

It was wonderful. It was almost too much. But Jules could cope. It was damned close to a dream come true.

Once he'd shed his various bits and bobs and changed into something more comfortable, Jules floated into the kitchen, and began preparing dinner. He always kept it simple on a Wednesday, so he was just cooking fresh spaghetti pasta and reheating the bolognaise sauce he'd made the night before. He felt more as if he should be preparing Grand Marnier Soufflé.

He replied to Archie and Jem's greetings as they arrived, he was sure he did, but eventually he became aware that Archie was saying, "Off in his own world again! It must be a fabulous place."

Jem snorted in her usual inelegant style. "Fabulous is exactly the right word. Reckon he's started reading a new romance novel by that Ewan guy."

Jules swivelled around to face them, and struck a 'manna is raining from heaven' pose. "It's better than that!"

Archie sat down and prepared himself for a fascinating tale. "Let's hear all about it, then!"

Jem groaned and sat, too, though she made a point of paying more attention to her phone as Jules launched into the story. He'd served up by the time he was done, and Archie and Jem were tucking into their meals while listening, more or less, to a summation of all the most delightful aspects.

"Well done, son," Archie said, "and well deserved."

"Deserved?" Jem protested, though not very vehemently. "He's being rewarded for doing something incredibly stupid."

"He's being rewarded for trying to fix a mistake he made, and for helping ensure others won't be tempted into the same trap."

"Meh," said Jem. "But, yeah, I guess. Congrats on the new client, anyway."

"Ta." Jules resolutely refused to let any of that take away the sparkle.

Archie gently encouraged, "Eat up, son."

Jules looked down at his own untouched dinner. The others were already halfway through theirs. And it looked delicious, if he did say so himself, but ... "I'm too happy to be hungry."

"Have a mouthful or two. It's very good."

Jules slowly obliged, though he had to mention again, "He remembered me, Dad. And not just 'cause of the red hair!"

"Of course. You're a very memorable person, Jules ... Handsome fellow, is he?"

Happiness billowed in Jules' chest. "He's *adorable* – but actually rather plain."

"Really?" Archie seemed surprised.

"I'm not quite as shallow as you think, obviously!"

"Tell me about him, then."

"He's slim, but doesn't really have a figure. He's plain, with light brown hair. He's pale, but not chalky white like me. And he has these amazing grey-green eyes that can just ..." Jules mimed taking a hit to the heart and ka-BOOM! "It's his eyes, and they're windows to the soul, right? And it's his heart and his mind, and his stories, and the way he writes, and the fact he believes in Happy Ever After ... *That's* what makes him so irresistible."

After a brief pondering, Archie asked, "Isn't he the bloke who was so active in the gay marriage campaign?"

"Yes," Jules replied with a grin.

Archie winked at him. "Sounds like you've found a good one there."

"Oh, Dad!" he protested.

"For God's sake, Archie, *please* don't give him ideas," said Jem.

"Why not? Celebrities are people, too, you know, and I think they appreciate being related to as such." Archie paused for a moment, as if about to say something, but then changing his mind. "Besides, this Ewan Byge fellow sounds all right. He might almost be good enough for our Jules. Almost."

Jem groaned and rolled her eyes.

Meanwhile Jules' imagination was running away with him … and Ewan was sliding a ring onto Jules' finger, his head bowed and his fine hazel-brown hair shifting like silk. Then he stood tall again, still holding Jules' hand, and the gaze of those beautiful sea-green eyes pierced Jules through the soul.

Six

Jules was still grinning a week later when he left the office to find – not unexpectedly – Leonard waiting for him on the pavement, in regular clothes again. "Mr Oakley's for a coffee?" Jules suggested as he walked up to Leonard.

"You took the words right out of my mouth," Leonard smoothly replied as he fell into step beside Jules.

"Of course, you're taking the risk that Daniel will assume we're dating."

Leonard glanced at him sidelong with that secretly pleased look of his. "If we were, Mr Madigan, I hope that you'd look even half as happy."

Jules bubbled over with laughter. He'd been doing that a lot lately. "My smile muscles are sore … and I have you to thank for it!"

"Ah, I suspect Mr Byge is the real reason for your good mood."

"But I never would have met him like that on my own. I never would have ended up working with him. And you're the one who made it happen, Leonard!"

They turned the corner and silently paced on for a few moments. Eventually Leonard said, "I suppose that I am, in a way. But the outcome has more to do with who you are, Jules."

Gosh. Well, Jules wasn't ready to ask for details about who he was. He didn't think he'd be game to even ask Archie about that. They paced on, until they reached the café, where Leonard was gentleman enough to let Jules open the door for him.

"Hello, Jules," Daniel called over. "Hello, Jules' new friend. Good to see you both again!"

Leonard took this in good part. "Hello, Daniel, and thank you. It's good to be back."

Jules' mobile rang at about ten on the Friday morning, and the display indicated it was the office, so Jules answered the call with a "Hello, Grace!"

"Hi, Jules honey. I've got one of your clients on the line, wants to speak with you. Okay if I put him through?"

"Yeah, that's fine."

"It's a Mr Byge."

Jules let out the kind of squeak that was usually only heard when squeezing plush toys. It would be particularly fitting for a plush turquoise dolphin, Jules thought.

A brief pause ensued.

Grace cautiously asked, "You want me to tell him you're unavailable? I can take a message. Or refer him to Bethany? Is there a problem, hon?"

"No problem," Jules managed. "No problem. That's fine." Stupidly, he leaned over so he could check how his hair looked in the reflective surface of the oven door. Then he cleared his throat, and made an effort to sound a bit manlier. "Thanks, Grace. You can put him through now."

"Well," she said doubtfully, "if you're sure."

"Of course I'm sure! Of course I'm sure! Good golly gosh, Grace, don't keep him waiting, he might have hung up by now!"

If Grace was a meaner person – like Jem, for instance – she might have put the call through while Jules was still wittering on. Thankfully, though, Jules only heard the click and the change in ambient noise once he was done. He took a breath, and said in what he hoped was something like his normal voice, "Hello, this is Jules Madigan."

"Hello, Jules!" said Ewan in bright tones, as if he was as happy to talk to Jules as Jules was to him. Which obviously couldn't actually be the case. "It's Ewan Byge. How are you?"

"I'm very well, thank you. How are you?"

"I'm great. I'm great. Well –" Ewan sighed. "To be honest, I'm completely overwhelmed by this spreadsheet you sent me."

"Oh. Really? It's the standard one that all our clients use. I set it up properly for you, I think ..." Jules tried to quickly open the thing up on his own laptop, despite him only having one hand available. "Hang on, I'm going to put you on speaker phone."

"So the whole office can hear me confessing to being a complete ignoramus?"

Jules chuckled. "No, you're in luck. I'm working from home today. And I don't even have a cat to judge you. It's just me here."

"Oh, all right." Ewan audibly relaxed a little. Jules hit the speaker button, and put the phone down – and was startled for all kinds of reasons when

Ewan continued in suggestive tones, "So, it's just you there …"

Jules laughed again, and tapped the volume control so Ewan wouldn't unintentionally boom. "Yes."

"Your boyfriend's out at work?"

His laughter was starting to become a bit nervous. Was he being flirted with by Ewan Byge Himself? "I, uh – I don't have a boyfriend."

"Husband?"

"None of those, uh, neither." Was that even grammatical? Did verbal flirting have to be grammatical? Jules knew people who'd knock back a date because someone had committed some kind of Cardinal Spelling Sin in a text message. "Um, okay, I'm looking at the spreadsheet here. Is there something specific you're having trouble with?"

"Yeah, just all of it!"

"Oh." Jules frowned, considering this, but he supposed that just because someone was super-intelligent about words didn't mean they were good with numbers. Jules himself could never write novels, after all. "How far did you get? Did you start with your bank statements?"

"I remember you telling me that, so that is indeed where I started … and that's where I failed, too."

"Okay, so are you looking at the spreadsheet now? It doesn't matter which month."

"Yes …"

"Start with your income, all the payments into your bank account. They need to have matching entries in the Invoices and Bankings sections at the top of the worksheet, yeah? Once you've got those sorted, then you can do your outgoings and expenses."

"Um … but I don't have invoices for everything. Not for royalties, anyway. Should I?"

Jules smiled at the mental image of Ewan scratching his head in the most adorable manner. "I guess you don't issue invoices, if you just receive your royalties directly from your agent."

"No, that's right. She makes the payments, and sends statements. I think."

"But you still need to make an entry for each amount of income under the Invoices section, and a matching entry in the Bankings section."

Ewan cleared his throat. "Okay, I do have invoices for some stuff, though."

"Yes?"

"I do this under a different name, and I'd rather it wasn't widely known, but I also do editing on a freelance basis."

"I see," Jules calmly responded – while inside he was a riot of glee. That was the first real secret he'd learned about Ewan Byge. It hadn't failed to occur to him that he'd be receiving insights into a narrow yet intriguing part of Ewan's life.

"You didn't know that, did you? Or did you?"

"No, I didn't, but I promise I'll be discreet." Jules paused for a moment, but then said it anyway. "I try to live my life like an open book, but that doesn't mean I don't respect other people's privacy."

"You're a good man, Jules Madigan."

Which was said with utter sincerity, but it was almost too much. It was too much.

After a quiet moment passed, Jules figured they'd better get back to business. He asked, "Can I share your screen, maybe, and we can work through a couple of examples on the spreadsheet?"

"Share my screen?" Ewan sounded distinctly unenthusiastic.

"Oh, I'm sorry," Jules blurted, abruptly remembering who they each were. "That's too much to ask. I wasn't thinking. I'm just a fan, I know. I know there's a line I can't cross."

"Just a fan?" Ewan echoed, now sounding amused, thank God. "Just a fan. That makes you one of my favourite people in all the world, darlin'. And you're my accountant now, too, don't forget that."

"Okay …"

"I was just – I don't even have the first clue about sharing a screen. If you mean my computer screen? Haven't got the first idea, Jules." He took a moment before adding, "You must be thinking I'm really quite stupid."

"Mr Byge," Jules quietly replied, "you write the most beautiful stories I've ever known. You're about as far from stupid as you could possibly be."

A sudden warmth grew between them, like a time-lapse film of a flower blooming, which Ewan just let sit there. Eventually he said, in exactly the same quiet tones, "Thank you very much, Jules."

"Sorry, I was afraid you thought I was being inappropriate."

"No," Ewan said, in what seemed his usual energetic manner. "No, not at all. In fact, I'm going to suggest something even more inappropriate still."

Jules sat there silent with his breath caught in his throat and his heart going pitterty-pat, pitterty-pat.

Ewan turned hesitant again. "I was wondering if you could possibly come over here, and do some of this for me."

Silence.

"I understand if that's not part of your actual job," Ewan rushed on. "But you'd be doing me an enormous favour – and I'd be happy to pay you, of course. Is that … Is that entirely out of the question?"

"Well," said Jules. "It's not exactly Standard Operating Procedure." He'd have to clear it with Bethany. It would have to be on his own time, and he was pretty sure he shouldn't accept any money for it, seeing as Ewan was already a client of the accountancy. He wondered if Bethany would dismiss the idea out of hand. But he'd have to tell her. Wouldn't he?

"No, I understand. I'll just have to muddle my way through –"

"Where's here?" Jules asked.

"Sorry, what?"

"When you say 'come over here', what exactly do you mean?"

Ewan let out a breath. "I mean my flat. Which is probably horribly inappropriate, you're right. But it's not my home … not my proper home."

His proper home? Jules envisaged a modest Georgian manor house amidst oaks and daffodils somewhere out in the Home Counties.

"I have a tiny little one-bedroom flat for when I'm in London, and that's where I keep all the business side of things."

"But it's where you live. Like, you didn't mean your agent's offices."

"It's where I live part-time," Ewan agreed. "This is going to be a problem, isn't it? I shouldn't have asked."

Jules saw the opportunity slipping away – and grabbed it with both hands. "No! No, I mean … I'm a *fan*, Ewan. Would you really trust me that far?"

Ewan chuckled warmly. "You have a conscience, Jules. You're one of the good guys."

"Oh," Jules managed.

"You know, I trust Leonard Edgar, I really do. Don't you?"

"Yes."

"Well, he sings your praises very highly, Jules. Very highly indeed."

An image flitted through Jules' head of Leonard very uprightly and dolefully singing about the unhappiness of a policeman's lot. He tried to smother a giggle. It didn't work. Which meant he kind of spluttered across the airwaves.

Ewan laughed to hear him. "You're thinking about our Leonard bursting into song, aren't you?"

"In a way," he confessed.

"I wonder if the City of London Police has a barbershop quartet," Ewan mused. "Wouldn't he look fine in a striped waistcoat and a boater?"

Jules spluttered some more. "Stop it!" he protested through the giggles. "Stop it!" But of course the reality was that he wanted Ewan to never stop.

"You're going to his *home*?" Jem demanded. It was apparent that, for once, Jules had managed to shock her.

"Yes," said Jules. "Tomorrow. Saturday."

"I *know* what day tomorrow is." She put her fork down with a clatter, and glared at him.

Jules gazed down at his own dinner. He'd made a fish pie served with garden peas. They always ate fish on a Friday, even though none of them was religious, not even Archie any more. Jules sighed, and wondered what he could do to divert Jem if dinner wouldn't do the job for him. He had no idea why she'd disapprove of him visiting Ewan, and he suspected that he didn't want to know, either.

Archie offered, "This could be a promising move in the right direction. Romantically speaking, I mean."

"Ha!" Jem cried. "I don't know why you're encouraging him. He obviously has *no* sense of judgement when it comes to this guy."

"I think you're being a tad unfair," Archie said. "It's not Ewan Byge who defrauded him. If anything, Ewan seems to be trying to make up for the situation. Which I have to say is rather decent of him."

"But going to his home? It's unprofessional, to say the least."

Jules decided he'd better head that one off at the pass. "I called Bethany and talked it over with her. She said she relies on me to be as scrupulous with this client as any of my others."

"Does she *know* how mad you are about him?"

Jules cleared his throat and shifted uncomfortably on his seat. "He came into the office when I wasn't expecting anything like that. I think she got a pretty good grasp on the situation."

Jem made a disgruntled kind of 'urgh' sound, and sat back a little. She picked up her fork, stabbed at her food for a moment – and then stabbed the fork in Jules' direction instead, complete with flying flecks of fish. "*Don't* let him take advantage of you."

In his own mind, Jules wistfully asked, 'What if I want to take advantage of him?' Out loud, though, Jules sniffed a little and muttered, "Chance would be a fine thing."

The next day – after too little sleep due to excitement, and too much anxiety over how to dress with deceptive casualness – Jules took the Tube to Islington. Ewan's flat was a fifteen-minute walk from the station, and a bewildering number of twisty streets away. Jules thanked the geeks of the world, yet again, for the sat nav in his phone.

Eventually, however, Jules stood in the pale sunshine on the pavement outside a Victorian terrace house not all that dissimilar to his own. The main difference was that this one had been converted into three flats, and it seemed that Ewan occupied the top floor.

Jules stared up at the front door with its peeling black paint and tarnished brass knob. He took a breath. "Do you even know what you're doing?" he asked himself – and he honestly had to answer, "Somehow I doubt it!"

He glanced down to inspect his blue jeans, grey-green jumper and white t-shirt. Everything seemed shipshape. He took another breath. And he climbed the few steps to the door, located the doorbell simply labelled 'THREE' and pressed it. A chime faintly sounded overhead. Then after a moment, Jules heard the footfalls of someone jogging down the stairs inside. Jules' heart tripped and then sped up to match the rhythm of Ewan Byge coming down to let Jules in.

Then the door was swinging open, and Ewan was Right There – grinning beautifully – and Jules simply wasn't ready for any of that. He opened his mouth, and basically managed to let out a gasp.

But Ewan didn't seem to even notice any of his foolishness. No doubt he was used to dealing with The Star-Struck. "Hello, Jules!" he cried. "How are you? Come on up, won't you?"

"Yes," said Jules. "Good. Yes. I mean, I'm good, thank you." By which time they were in the hallway, and Ewan was shutting the front door behind them. "How are you?"

"I'm great!" Ewan led the way up the stairs. "You've no idea how much I appreciate you taking this on. It's such a load off my mind!"

"Oh. Well." Jules frowned. "I'm sure you'll find it straightforward enough once I get you going."

Ewan opened the door to his flat, and ushered Jules in – taking the opportunity to aim a seductive glance Jules' way as he passed. "I wouldn't count on it. I may never let you leave again."

The door closed behind them, and Jules shivered with a moment's apprehension. He was too busy, however, looking around him curiously at Ewan's home. Or, at least, his home away from home. "Do you write here?" Jules asked. "It's weird, but we live in a house just like this – except that the stairs are in different places, not all in one spiral like here. But we're in my bedroom!"

That drew a filthy chuckle. "Are we now?"

This room, however, was a combination of kitchenette and living room. Jules snuck a look through the open doorway into the other room at the back of the house. "I guess you sleep in Jemima's room!"

The chuckle modulated to an appreciative murmur. "I'm sure she's lovely, but I think I know which I'd prefer …"

Jules was blushing by now, which wasn't good. He could feel the heat of it on his cheekbones – and he knew how awful he looked with red splotches bright on his pale skin. So he put his head down, and headed for the laptop already set up on a small table, with a box haphazardly full of paperwork beside it. Jules cleared his throat. "So, I guess this is it, then?"

"This is it." Ewan was immediately focused on business again. He walked over to lay his hands on the box, as if feeling it to be a heavy burden. "This is all the stuff for the current year that Ted brought over. If you can help me sort it out …"

As he sat down at the laptop, Jules dared to look at the man again. "Of course I can."

Ewan grinned at him. "Coffee, then, to help you through?"

"You must have read my mind," Jules replied with great satisfaction.

It took Jules just over two hours to transfer the year-to-date figures into the spreadsheet, sense-checking it as he went. Brother-in-law Ted had obviously known what he was doing. Jules commentated as he went, trying to help Ewan understand his own finances – but the man obviously didn't want to engage.

"Not so long ago," he explained, "I hardly even knew what a spreadsheet was. I'm on a steep learning curve, Jules. Be patient with me!"

Jules was sympathetic, of course, but Ewan was horribly restless. He wandered around fetching coffee and snacks, answering calls and messages on his phone, picking things up and then putting them down, and talking. He'd answer any questions Jules put to him about his accounts, but then Ewan would come back with questions of his own.

"Which is your favourite romance novel?"

Jules grinned. That was easy. "*The 'True Love' Solution*, of course."

Ewan let out a guffaw, though he was obviously pleased. "I didn't mean which you liked of mine. I meant your favourite overall."

"Oh! Well, in that case I guess my favourite would be … *The 'True Love' Solution*."

The guffaw became a real laugh. "You're a sweetheart, Jules."

Jules couldn't restrain himself from asking, "Is there going to be more? I mean, tell me to mind my own business if you like, of course – but I love it so much. Is there going to be a sequel, or a series?"

"D'you want more? I kinda thought the story was complete."

"Oh no … I want to know all about what Dexter and Mike get up to on the *True Love*. I want to read more about their Happy Ever After. And Tracy and Liz were pretty cute, too. They're gonna have so much fun together."

Ewan wandered over to stand there with folded arms, considering Jules with an assessing gaze. "Do you think they'd marry? Dexter and Mike, I mean."

Jules didn't have to ponder that for very long. "Actually, I don't think they would. I think they'd be absolutely committed to the relationship, they'd put all their faith in each other, but they'd enjoy the feeling of freedom too much."

"I think you're right," Ewan agreed with a grin, those arms falling loose again. "They are both a tad … unconventional, aren't they?"

"Mmm …" Jules agreed in appreciative tones.

"Well, I'll have to see what I can do …" Ewan turned and paced away again, as far as he could within the room. "I can see them out on the ocean together, you know. That feeling of freedom, like you said. And now I can see the sun sparkling on the surface of the sea, and I can feel the salt wind in my hair. … If I write it, it'll be for you, Jules."

That was as thrilling as slicing through the waves on a yacht with your true love, or perhaps even more so.

"I'm assuming your visit to Ewan's went well," Archie quietly said that evening when it was just him and Jules on the sofa with their feet up. The telly burbled on in the background. "Judging by the way you've been smiling ever since, I guess it went very well indeed."

"Yes, it was wonderful." Jules confessed, "I really like him, Dad. I know he's way out of my league, but …"

"But nothing, Jules. We're all human, even Ewan Byge. Even –"

Jules nudged Archie with an elbow when it seemed he wouldn't continue. "Come on, out with it."

Archie cast him an uncertain look, but then confessed, "There's a woman at the care home. One of our residents – she's over ninety now, bless her, and quite frail. She used to be on the stage. You've probably never heard of her, but she was quite the star in my day."

Jules was grinning. "Have you got yourself a girlfriend, Dad?"

"Oh, no. Heavens, no. But she enjoys me playing the gallant, and we've become fast friends. These things aren't impossible, Jules."

"I've noticed you've been extra happy lately. I'm so glad for you."

"I'm glad for me, too," Archie responded with a smile. "And for you, Jules. Never think you're not worthy. Especially not *you*, my precious Jewels."

And in that moment, Jules could almost put his full faith in the possibilities.

Seven

Jules was still grinning on the last Wednesday of September when he found Leonard waiting for him yet again. "This is already a habit," Jules remarked. "How many times before it becomes a tradition?"

Leonard barely managed a distracted smile for the thought. He was looking very intense. "I've interviewed the suspect," he said. "Sorry. Jules, I have some news," Leonard announced as if starting over. "I interviewed the suspect in his home. I seized his computer equipment, and other evidence."

"Oh!" said Jules. And quickly sobered. He contemplated this for a long moment, staring down at the pavement, trying to work out what he felt. "Oh."

"It's good news, isn't it? He admitted the fraud. There were other victims, too, Jules. He's been arrested and formally charged with a number of offences."

"Oh."

"He's been released on bail, but I don't think we'll need to wait too long for the court hearing."

"I see."

Leonard considered him very carefully. "Jules? What's wrong?"

Jules lifted his head, and offered Leonard a smile, though he knew it was a bit weak. He gave himself a shake. "Let's go get a coffee, shall we?"

"Of course." And Leonard silently escorted Jules two blocks down and one across to Mr Oakley's Coffee House.

They walked in and settled at what had become their usual booth. They must have looked quite pensive, as Daniel's face fell when he saw them. He didn't make a comment, though, but just took their order and filled it as quickly as possible.

Once it was just the two of them, with their coffees sitting untouched between them, Leonard asked again, "What's wrong? I thought you'd be pleased. Are you worried that –"

"I'm sure *you're* pleased," Jules offered. "You've done a terrific job!"

"Jules –"

"An arrest already, that's fantastic."

"You might not even need to go to court as a witness. He's already admitted the crime; it's more than likely he'll plead guilty at the court hearing, and then the case will move directly to sentencing."

"It's not that. Not really." Jules grimaced unhappily. "I'm brave enough to stand in the witness box, I think."

"You *are* brave," Leonard said in low and surprisingly fervent tones.

"Am I? Well, my Dad says so, too, sometimes, though I suppose he has to. But, you know … this is the first time ever – in my whole life – that I've deliberately set out to make an enemy." He shot a pleading glance at the police officer, who must be made of far bolder stuff. "And this is serious, too. The guy might go to prison or whatever. I mean, obviously not just for my case, but you say there are others he's defrauded … It's not like I've posted a one-star review for a book – and I don't even do that!" Jules sighed. "There. You probably think I'm a complete cowardly custard."

"Not in the slightest. Quite the opposite."

"Well –"

"If you're worried – I can assure you that very few defendants try to harass the victims or witnesses. Very few indeed. It adds to the drama of television shows, of course, but in reality –"

"That's not the point," said Jules.

"No, the point is that *I'll protect you*. I mean, you'll be protected. If you're called to court, you'll be kept away from the defendant and his family or friends. And he won't have sight of your address or anything like that."

Jules gestured helplessly. "He already has my address. I sent it to him for delivery of the manuscript page, and the typewriter."

"But I seized his computer as evidence, and I didn't find much paperwork at his home. He may no longer have access to that information."

"It's not like it's a state secret," Jules argued. "He could find out easily enough. I'm registered to vote, for a start! But anyway, I suppose he'd be an idiot to try anything, wouldn't he?"

"*Yes*," said Leonard, looking fierce. "I'd bring the full weight of the law to bear upon him."

A thrill electrified Jules, zapping down his backbone and prickling the hairs on his nape. The two of them stared at each other across the table. Leonard's dark eyes were so fuckin' intense … The moment resounded with possibilities.

Which was, of course, when Jules' phone rang. He growled a little at the intrusion.

But it was the ringtone he'd assigned to Archie, so he muttered, "Sorry, that's my Dad," and picked up the call. "Hello."

"Hello, Jules," Archie greeted him in slightly harried tones. Usually they exchanged a 'How are you?' or 'How's your day?' but this time Archie continued right on. "I just wanted to warn you that the boiler's stopped working – it probably broke down early this morning, and we just didn't realise. The problem is that the landlord's not answering her phone, and we haven't found a plumber yet who'll be available before the weekend."

"Oh bugger," said Jules.

"So we're going to be a bit chilly tonight, and there'll be no hot water."

"Oh buggerations."

"Once you get home, we'll just order pizza for dinner, all right? We can boil a kettle for the washing up, but let's avoid making too much extra work for ourselves tonight."

"Yes, yes, of course. I'll come home now."

Leonard had been watching with a growing frown. "What's wrong?" he asked.

"Hang on, Dad, I'm with Leonard." Jules shifted the phone away from his mouth but not his ear, and started, "The boiler –"

"The policeman?" Archie blurted. "Sorry, I didn't mean to interrupt your date."

Jules groaned, and replied, "It's not a –" But then he thought better of finishing that sentence out loud. "Hang on, Dad, just let me tell Leonard." He lowered the phone and explained, "The boiler's not working, and we're having trouble finding a plumber. You wouldn't know anyone, would you?"

Leonard was nodding, and then tapped his own chest. "I might be able to help. If you'll allow me?"

"Really?"

"It's not that I'm qualified or anything, but my grandfather was the maintenance man at my school, and he could fix anything. He wanted 'better' things for me, but I learned what I could from him."

A grin ambushed Jules, and he lifted the phone again. "Dad, I'm bringing Leonard home with me. Sounds like he's our answer. Make that pizza for four."

"You'd better let me earn it first," Leonard protested as they slid out of the booth.

The boiler was in the big basement room, which was Archie's, and there was also a tank in the attic. Once Jules had introduced his friend to Archie and Jem, they all headed downstairs to stare with arms crossed and pensive looks at the boiler. Leonard said, "I was going to ask if it's still under warranty, as I wouldn't want to void it, but I assume not?"

"Maybe it was," Archie agreed, "back when I was a lad. But there's no need to worry about that sort of thing, Constable. Any help you can give will be very welcome."

"All right," Leonard replied in distracted tones. Then he started investigating the problem, both upstairs and down, obviously working through a mental checklist.

Jem went up to the kitchen to make a round of teas and coffees, while Archie produced his own toolbox and then went round to the neighbours when Leonard required more. Jules pretty much just hovered uselessly.

They were all still in their coats and scarves – and her hat, in Jem's case – although Leonard stripped off his coat once he started the actual work needed. Archie commented, "It's shocking how quickly this house loses its heat. We really ought to think about insulation."

"I'll soon have this sorted out, Mr Madigan."

"You will? That's wonderful! Thank you, Constable Edgar."

"Leonard is fine. I'm not here in an official capacity. I'm just a friend."

Archie glanced at Jules with more meaning than was warranted, and ignored Jules rolling his eyes in response. "Then, Leonard, please call me Archie."

"Thank you, Archie." Leonard paused and sat back on his heels. "I'll show you the problem, if you like. Well, there's two problems, and one has triggered the other. I can only manage a temporary fix, but that will see you through until you can get a proper plumber here."

"We're very grateful, Leonard." Archie went to crouch by Leonard, and the talk rapidly descended into valves and various kinds of thermostats.

Jules took that as his cue to head upstairs to hang out with Jem. She was sitting in her regular place at the kitchen table. "Looks like he's getting it fixed," Jules told her.

"You found a good one there. A real little homemaker."

"Yeah, yeah." He sat beside her at the table, and peered at the pizza menu in her hands. "Have you ordered yet? I don't think Dad and Leonard will be long now."

"What sort of pizza does your cop like?"

"He's not *my* anything!" Jules protested. "And I don't know. We've only ever had coffee together."

"I bet … with a scrawny figure like that … he'll want healthy."

Jules huffed a breath. "He is *not* scrawny! He's *fit*. I bet he runs marathons or something."

"So, a primavera pizza, maybe with chicken."

"Anyway, I think you're wrong."

"Never. But go right ahead and amuse me."

"If you ask him about the pizza, he'll just say, 'Whatever you're having, thank you.'"

Jem snorted. But Jules was confident he'd read Leonard correctly.

A popping in the radiators preceded a gurgling and a ticking, and then within moments Jules and Jem could feel the first hint of warmer air. Archie and Leonard appeared soon after, looking pretty pleased with themselves. "Leonard's fixed it!" Archie announced rather redundantly.

"Temporarily, at least," Leonard clarified.

"You're a miracle worker," Jem said. "What sort of pizza do you want?"

"Oh," said Leonard, clasping his hands together for a moment. "A slice of whatever you're having will be fine, thank you."

Jules cast Jem a smug glance – but her snort and her knowing look undermined his triumph. Somehow she'd got the idea that …

The pizza place was on speed dial, so Jem had the order placed moments later. Archie fetched the spare chair and invited Leonard to sit – next to Jules, of course, seeing as Jules had the long side of the table. Jules promptly stood and made them another round of hot drinks, and set out plates, cutlery and napkins. The radiators were all coming to life, but the house was still way too chilly. The four of them finally settled around the table, still in their coats, and with their hands wrapped around the steaming mugs of tea or coffee.

After a long moment of silence, Archie said, "You'll have to come for dinner on another night of the week, Leonard. Jules usually cooks for us, when he doesn't have to go into the office, and he's a dab hand at it."

Could his Dad *be* any more embarrassing? "I just make simple stuff. Nothing to boast about."

"It's always delicious," Archie stoutly continued, "and nutritious, too."

"I'm sure it is," Leonard obligingly agreed.

Jules said, "Chicken, sage and mushroom pie tomorrow. Anyone could make it."

"No, they couldn't, son," Archie insisted.

"I love pie," Leonard remarked.

Jem snorted again. "Well, *that* could be a problem."

Jules was possibly the only one to understand the reference – or at least he certainly hoped that Archie wasn't across such slangy terms for the Lady Parts, and he suspected it wasn't exactly Leonard's area of expertise. Jules shot Jem a venomous look anyway.

She said in suspiciously sweet tones, "Jules will make someone the perfect husband one day."

"Oh my God, *shut up*, would you?"

"My son is rather a romantic, Leonard, and of course Jemima teases him dreadfully."

"What else are sisters for?" Jem opined.

"Be careful," Jules said, "she bites."

"Only consensually."

"We're not *really* sister and brother. We couldn't be any more different. She's poly, you see."

"Polly?" Leonard echoed. "Oh, I see. Poly-what?"

"Poly-everything, thank you," Jem retorted. "Sexuality, gender – it's all far more fluid than most people dare to dream of."

Jules said, "Maybe omni is a better description. As in omnivorous."

"Hey, at least I have my dignity, you know. Far more than you do."

Archie interrupted them in heavy tones. "Children, we have a guest. A grown-up guest."

Leonard looked a tad self-conscious, but offered, "It's a compliment, really … that they don't feel they have to be on their best behaviour."

"You may live to regret that thought."

They were saved by the doorbell. Archie went down to collect the pizza, while Jules got up to fetch the lemonade and ginger beer from the fridge. "What would you like to drink, Leonard? I'll make you another coffee, if you like. We only have these for cold drinks – the old-fashioned versions, yeah? I know not everyone likes them – but otherwise it's milk or water."

"The ginger beer, thank you," Leonard replied. "That's quite a treat!"

Jules set the bottle down nearby him without making eye contact, and went to get four glasses. Then Archie brought the pizzas to the table, and everyone was cheerfully distracted for a while. Jem had ordered two large pizzas, and a good half of each had disappeared before anyone said anything more than 'Please', 'Thank you', 'God, this is good' and 'I may not die of hypothermia after all'.

The remaining slices were devoured in a slightly more civilised manner. Jules had time to ponder the situation while Archie and Leonard exchanged pleasantries in between mouthfuls. Archie and Jem had obviously leapt to all kinds of conclusions, which wasn't exactly fair on poor Leonard – who didn't deserve to be rigorously match-made to someone like Jules just because Leonard was nice enough to help where he could. In any case, there was Ewan Byge to consider, and Jules really had to wonder how Archie and Jem could possibly forget that.

"I went to Ewan Byge's flat on Saturday," Jules commented out of the blue as the eating frenzy was finally ending with a whimper.

Leonard was obviously surprised, but he didn't say anything. He simply turned to consider Jules carefully. Archie was silent. Jem watched them all with narrowed eyes.

"I went to help him with his accounts, his paperwork."

There was the slightest hint of relaxation in his companions.

"I guess, just because he's great with words doesn't mean he's good with numbers! I'm no good with words, after all. So Ewan and me ... we kind of ... dovetail."

Leonard went a little pale.

Jem chuckled with a wry note, and said quietly, "Is *that* what they're calling it these days?"

"But there's one thing we agree on, and that's Marriage Equality. He was such a huge part of that campaign. He still has a poster up on his wall."

There was nothing more than an 'uh huh' kind of response from anyone, so Jules sailed blithely on.

"In fact, his London flat is in a house just like this one, and his living room and kitchen is in my bedroom here. ... So to speak."

Another silence threatened to de-rail the whole evening, but eventually Leonard said, "I read one of his books. As part of my investigation." He cleared his throat, and amended, "As a result of my investigation. You made me curious," Leonard added to Jules. "So I bought a copy of *The 'True Love' Solution*."

"Oh, that's marvellous!" Jules cried. "Did you enjoy it?"

A slight pause, as if Leonard was considering the diplomatic answer. "I don't think I've ever read a romance, so I have nothing to compare it with. But it was very engaging. I never wanted to put it down."

"Excellent!" Jules almost clapped his hands in glee. "What did you think about –"

"That's my cue to make the tea," said Jem. "Leonard?"

"Yes, please. Milk and sugar, if I may."

"Of course." Jem went to put the kettle on, and Archie settled back in his seat as if ready to listen or let it all flow over him, as it suited.

Jules continued to Leonard, "Ewan always writes Happy Ever Afters. Maybe one or two Happy For Nows, but almost always HEAs. So, what did you think about Liz and Tracy getting married at the end, but Dexter and Mike just sailing off into the metaphorical sunset?"

Leonard looked a bit mystified, as if not at all sure about how he should answer.

Jules helped him out. "Ewan asked me if I thought Dexter and Mike would marry, too, but actually I think they're happiest the way they are. Together by choice, and kind of free at the same time."

Dead silence.

Archie said, "You astonish me, son."

"Yeah, where did that come from?" Jem chipped in. "You're all about the wedding bells, Jules."

"Marriage isn't for everyone," he loftily declared.

"But it's what you've always dreamed of," Archie persisted, "and they're your favourite fictional couple. Aren't they?"

Which was all true. Jules sniffed, and was lost for how to explain himself. What was the point he'd been trying to make?

Jem brought over the cups of tea, while Archie belatedly began tidying away the remains of dinner. They all finally shrugged off their coats and let them hang off the back of their chairs.

Leonard tried to get the conversational ball rolling again. "Jemima, if you're so very different to Jules, what do you think about Marriage Equality?"

"It's Jem, mate, unless you're arresting me."

"I apologise. Jem."

"Well, actually I approve."

Leonard obliged her by looking surprised.

"Not because *I* want to marry. I don't even want to be monogamous – despite all the sods who tell me I just haven't met That Special Someone. I've actually found a few special someones over the years, and I can tell you that Friends with Benefits works just fine."

"Why do you approve of 'gay marriage', then?" he prompted.

"Because it frees things up, doesn't it? It recognises that relationships are more about choice and love than convention and reproduction. And once no one is gonna decide which gender you can marry, or which sexuality fits, which romantic leanings are acceptable, then it really doesn't matter any more, does it? Only to the individual. And that's how it should be."

Leonard was smiling his quietly happy smile. "I like that," he said. "I like that very much."

"Good," said Jem.

Another silence stretched as they sipped their tea, but it was comfortable now. Neither Archie nor Jem asked about Leonard's views or preferences, as they seemed to assume they knew very well. They assumed it involved Jules. Obviously Leonard would set his sights far higher, though. He'd want someone more serious and less flibbertigibbet. Not that Jules minded because … well, Ewan Byge.

Jules' musings and the general peace were soon broken, of course.

"Wait a minute!" cried Jem. "You're not telling me your writing bloke sleeps in my bedroom, are you?" She shuddered. "We'll have to swap, Jules!"

"What do you care?" he asked. "Given the great variety of people who've slept in your actual bedroom?"

"My brother's Number One Crush in my bed? No, thanks!"

When it came time for Leonard to go, Archie and Jem each said their farewells very nicely, and then pointedly left it for Jules to see him to the door. For Leonard's sake, Jules fulfilled this duty without seeming too grudging. In the little hallway, as Leonard organised himself into his coat and scarf and gloves, Jules said, "Thank you. Really. Thank you so much for helping us tonight."

"It was my pleasure. Thank you for having me stay for dinner. And for introducing me to your family. Archie and Jem are –" Leonard paused for a moment, apparently judging just how far to go. "Well, I'd say you're very lucky, Jules, but you deserve to have such people in your life, and I'm very glad you do."

"Oh." Jules felt a sharp pang of sympathy. He hardly dared ask about Leonard's situation, especially as he knew Leonard lived at the police section house – alone in a crowd, in effect. "That's kind of you." On an impulse, he issued the invitation that he hadn't meant to. "Come on another night – I mean any night but Wednesday – and I'll cook you dinner. Your favourite dinner, if you have one, and your favourite pudding, too."

Leonard smiled in what was, for him, a broad grin. "Thank you! I'd appreciate that very much."

"Good. Well, you have my number, so just let me know when you're available. When your shifts allow you an evening off, or whatever."

"I will." Leonard was fully dressed now for the chilly evening outside, but he still stood there immovably, with his hands firmly in his coat pockets. "You can let me earn it again, if you will. Am I right that Archie lives in the basement room?"

Jules felt his brow crease in confusion. "Yes?"

"I was thinking that a fresh coat of paint would help liven it up again. I'm sure you already have plans, and I don't mean to intrude, but I could help with that. If you and I pitched in – and Jem as well, if she likes – we could get it done in a day."

"Oh." Jules just shrivelled up inside. He was a bad son. "Oh, you're right. It is horribly dingy down there. You see," he pleaded, "before Dad came to live with us, the Flatmate from Hell had that room, and you'll understand we didn't make much of an effort on his behalf."

"I'm glad that you have Archie here instead now."

"But you're right. I should have thought to make it a bit nicer." He was a bad bad son, there was no doubt about that.

Leonard's face had fallen about as far as Jules'. "I didn't mean to criticise! I apologise. I should mind my own business." Reaching for the door handle, Leonard said, "Thank you again for a lovely evening. I'm sorry I've ended it on an unpleasant note."

"You didn't! You didn't. You're right to criticise, if that's even what it was." Jules nodded. "Let me talk to the others, though I'm sure they'd be very happy about the idea. If you're free on a Saturday or Sunday, we could make a day of it, as you say. It'll be fun."

"Yes," said Leonard with a smile. "That's what I thought, too."

"And Dad does deserve to have a nice room."

"Yes," said Leonard – and for a moment Jules thought he might push in and press a consolation kiss to Jules' cheek or something. But he didn't. Leonard simply met Jules' gaze, and said "Goodnight" very softly, and then let himself out.

Jules closed the door after him, and then leaned back against it. Apparently, despite himself, he'd made a new friend. Or maybe Leonard just had a thing for lame ducks.

Eight

The following Saturday saw Jules standing once more outside the house which contained Ewan's flat. This time his deceptively casual outfit involved faded black jeans, a green t-shirt, and a jumper made from a tweedy brown yarn that included flecks of greens and blues. The sun was shining, but a cool breeze rustled dry autumn leaves along the pavement so they made a pitterty-pat, pitterty-pat sound, like a tripping heartbeat.

It seemed that even more of the black paint on the front door had peeled away, revealing a motley remnant of other lives. Jules laughed under his breath. "Has anyone who ever stood here known what they were doing? Probably not!"

After another long moment, Jules climbed up to the door, and rang the bell for flat three. A faint chime was followed gratifyingly quickly by Ewan's footsteps jogging down the stairs. Ewan Byge! Ewan Byge welcoming Jules into his home. Well, not his *real* home, but Jules wasn't complaining.

And then suddenly, gloriously Ewan was there at the door, beaming at him and crying "Hello, Jules!" – and really Jules had nothing to complain about at all, everything to be grateful for. "It's great to see you again. How are you? Come on in, won't you?"

"I'm good, thanks," Jules said as he followed Ewan up the stairs, trying not to trip over his own feet as his greedy gaze caressed the sweet curves of Ewan's rear, tantalisingly hinted at under comfortably loose blue denim. "Well, actually I'm great!"

"So you are," Ewan said, glancing back at exactly the wrong moment and catching Jules checking him out. Thank goodness Ewan just chuckled, and blithely announced, "I've already got the coffee brewing!"

"Oh, that's good," Jules managed faintly in response. Then they were inside the flat, and Jules put aside his embarrassment in the fuss of sorting himself out and settling at the table with the laptop, while Ewan headed for the kitchenette and fetched two mugs down from a high cabinet … Jules tried not to notice the glimpse of narrow belly between jeans and t-shirt as Ewan reached up.

Jules was there to enter the figures for September into Ewan's spreadsheet, and show Ewan how to do it for himself the following month. It was soon all too obvious that Ewan really wasn't interested in learning, though, or at least not about accountancy. Jules diligently worked away, taking his time and commentating as he went in the hope of something catching hold of Ewan's attention. He wasn't overly successful.

As Jules took a moment's break to drink his coffee, Ewan dropped into the chair nearby, considered him with a bright speculative gaze, and said, "I bet I can guess your favourite colour, Jules."

Jules smiled, and lifted the mug to his mouth, half-hiding behind it. "Can you?"

"Yes, I think I can …" That gaze swept over him, and then over him again, like a curious caress. "Your favourite colour, Jules Madigan, is … green."

He burst out laughing, partly because Ewan was absolutely right and partly because it was perfectly obvious. "Too easy!" Jules protested. "It's the best colour to go with my red hair."

"Aw …" Ewan moaned in mock disappointment. "It's not because of my green eyes?"

Jules dared to glance at said eyes – and then put his coffee down and tried to take refuge in the accountancy work. "It's been my favourite colour ever since I was old enough to realise I was meant to like blue because I was a boy."

"Always the rebel, weren't you, Jules?" Ewan asked in affectionately rhetorical tones.

Affectionate … ? Jules was too alarmed to know how best to answer, so he reached for the next expenses receipt. "And this is from Staples superstore for … notepads, a box of A4 paper, printer ink, folders and pens."

"Her Majesty's Tax Collectors can hardly argue with that deduction for a writer, can they?"

"Only the most obtuse!" Jules started typing. "See, it's just a matter of putting in the date of the receipt and a description of what it is. Then you enter the amount either in the Company Bank Account column, or the Cash Expenses column, depending on how you paid for it. Then you enter it again in the right column for that type of expenses … the Postage and Stationery column, in this case. And that's it!"

Ewan sighed, and his focus was obviously elsewhere. After a moment,

Ewan quietly commented, "You intrigue me, Jules Madigan."

Jules picked up the next receipt with fingers that trembled. "How's that?" he asked in what he hoped were the lightest of tones.

"You're so into all this, aren't you?" Ewan cast a dispirited gesture at the paperwork and the spreadsheet and everything involved with his accounts.

"I guess so …" Jules frowned over this for a moment. "I mean, I'm not 'into it' like I'm into reading romance novels … and yours in particular. But I like the work. I like putting the effort in to make it all work out neatly and correctly." He sighed in his turn. "Does that make me very boring?"

"Not in the slightest," Ewan immediately countered. "That's why I'm intrigued, do you see? Because when I think green, I think … life and hope and … springtime." Ewan had drawn closer to him. "*That's* why I guessed green for you."

Jules was barely breathing. "You don't think … passion?"

"No, *red* is for passion," Ewan insisted, casting a fiery glance at Jules' hair.

A still moment between them held and held … It could go either way. It honestly could. If Jules turned his head into Ewan's orbit, they'd be almost perfectly aligned, Ewan would lean in and kiss him, and … astonishingly … Jules might win all he'd ever dreamed of. So why was he hesitating?

Well, he reflected, Jules was a fan of Ewan the author, and Ewan was the client of Jules the accountant. Could it *be* any more awkward? And actually Jules really couldn't quite believe that Ewan wanted him, not the real *him*, despite all this talk of green for life and red for passion. This was just a moment's confused proximity. And after all, Ewan was hesitating, too. He must have known that Jules was his for the taking. And yet he did not take. Well, Jules thought.

He let out a quiet breath, and turned his head away. Just the very slightest amount.

And Ewan just as quietly drew back, and then stood. Wandered aimlessly off a couple of paces. Put his hands on his hips and considered something in the kitchen. Maybe the coffee pot.

Jules picked up the next receipt, though he found his eyes wouldn't focus on it enough to read the details.

After another moment dragged by, Ewan cleared his throat, and announced, "I've been thinking of that sequel you wanted. About Dexter and Mike."

"Uh huh," Jules managed.

"I've got the title already." Ewan let a beat go by. "*Sensational.*"

Jules cleared his throat, and turned to offer Ewan an uncomplicated smile. "Thank you. That's absolutely perfect."

"There was a moment," Jules whispered to Jem that evening over the dinner table, while they waited on an unusually tardy Archie to clean up and sit down. "There was a moment today … in which Ewan Byge almost kissed me." He sat back and boggled at her.

She boggled back, though with a slightly sardonic air. "Almost?"

"We were *thiiis* close," Jules said, holding his thumb and forefinger a hair's breadth apart.

"So why didn't you? It's not like you to be faint-hearted in the winning of a fair fellow."

Jules sat back and huffed. "It's complicated! There are ethics involved."

"Yeah, right," she drawled.

He could hardly help but bite. "I know you – and *you* wouldn't care about conflicts of interest."

"That is so entirely beside the point! Don't make *that* your excuse."

A moment ground by. Jules decided to ask. "What is the point, then?"

"I know you, Jules – and *you* don't realise what a great catch you are."

"Oh, really!" he retorted. "And what would you know about that? You're not looking to catch or be caught. So why should I trust *your* opinion?"

That was when Archie finally showed up. "I'm sorry," he offered, easing into his seat. "You should have started."

"Of course we wouldn't start without you," Jules replied in tones that were still a bit constricted with irritation. Which Archie definitely didn't deserve. Jules smiled at him, and began serving up a plate for Jem. "Lamb chops today." Which was stating the obvious. "Your favourite, Dad," he added.

"Thank you, Jewels." Archie paused for a moment.

Jules passed Jem her plate, and then started on one for Archie.

Finally, Archie said, "I heard the tail-end of that. Were you talking about Leonard?"

"No," Jules immediately replied, shooting a quelling glance at Jem. "Not at all." Though it occurred to him with some relief that there was one

Leonard-related topic he should have brought up by now. "But speaking of Leonard, he's going to let me know next time he has a free day on a weekend, and we're going to paint your room, Dad. Brighten it up a bit."

Archie looked surprised, and glanced from Jules to Jem and back again as if seeking answers.

"It is rather dingy down there," Jules continued.

"That's a kind thought, Jules," Archie managed. "Thank you!"

He sighed, and confessed. "It's Leonard you should thank. It was his idea. I, uh … I should have thought of it myself, Dad. We could have made it a bit more welcoming for you when you moved in."

"Yes," said Jem, obviously feeling as chagrined as Jules. "I'll help. Clean the windows, let some more light in. And the window well out the front must have about ten years of dead leaves and litter in it. I'll get that cleared out, too."

"This is very good of you," said Archie. "I should have done some cleaning myself!"

"No, no, no," the two of them protested. Heavens, Jules felt about half an inch tall. He couldn't even take proper care of his own darling Dad. There really was something wrong with him.

They ate their dinner for a while, in a thoughtful silence.

Eventually Archie commented, "Leonard is a good man, Jules."

"True," Jules admitted. Leonard was a good man indeed – and really truly far too good for Jules, but he knew he'd only be asking for an argument if he said as much. Instead he turned to Jem, and said, "Of course this raises the question of how long we're going to be here, and how much we spend on this place versus how much we put towards a deposit."

That successfully distracted Jem at least. Her eyes sparked, and she sat up from her usual post-meal slouch. "Ah, sweet Ginger Nut! Are you on board with my plans, then?"

"Yes," Jules said – though he had to admit to himself that it was more because he felt it was inevitable than because he really *wanted* to. "I guess if we're making an offer on this place, then we've got plenty of reasons for doing it up."

Jem narrowed her gaze. "But if we go too far then the landlord will put the price up, won't she?"

Archie tilted his head in consideration. "I don't think clean windows and a lick of paint is going to have much of an effect on the property value. From what I've read, that sort of thing might help it sell quicker, but won't greatly affect the actual price."

Jem grinned. "You've been researching this, Archie?"

"Of course! Anything I can do to help either or both of you –"

Jules reached across to grasp Archie's hand where it rested on the table.

"Well, then," Archie concluded, "any small things we can do to make this place more liveable, we should go ahead with. Otherwise –"

"I'm going to set up a special savings account for our deposit!" Jem announced.

And so it was decided.

Not that it was what mattered most to Jules. What mattered most to Jules was Ewan Byge. He was still buzzing a few days later. That moment in which Ewan had almost kissed him was still with Jules, and in his imagination he forgot scruples and leant in towards the man, and was met with a Real Life True Love Kiss, the reality of all those kisses Ewan had written about over the years. All that tender pleasure must have been felt by Ewan, all that lush passion must have been experienced by him. And Jules … oh Jules would have all the benefit of it.

Jules emerged from the office on the Wednesday evening to, not unexpectedly, find Leonard waiting for him. For the sake of being tactful, Jules tried to damp down the thrum of the Ewan-related UST, but he knew he'd only be partially successful.

"You look happy," said Leonard in greeting. He quirked an eyebrow, looking for all the world like a detective in an old black-and-white film. "I surmise you've visited Mr Byge again."

"You surmise correctly," Jules said with a grin as they turned and headed off towards Mr Oakley's. "But never mind that. How are you, Leonard? Have you had a good week?"

Leonard glanced at him, perhaps a little surprised. This must have been about the first time Jules had expressed an interest. Which made Jules a bad friend as well as a bad son. "I'm well, thank you," Leonard replied. "And it has been a good week. Busy, but that's the way it should be."

"Excellent."

They turned the corner and paced on together. Eventually Leonard said, "You don't ask about the case. You don't ask what progress I've made."

Jules pondered that for a moment and then offered an apologetic shrug. "I guess it doesn't … feel as if it's my business any more."

Leonard cast him a worried look. "I have other evidence as well. Other people are involved. But you're an important witness, Jules."

"That's okay. I'll do whatever you need me to, Leonard." They paused outside the door to Mr Oakley's, unwilling to interrupt the conversation. "I guess I just felt that … once I'd given my statement, it was out of my hands. You know?"

Leonard nodded, though it seemed more to indicate he was listening rather than he was agreeing.

"I'd been worrying about it that whole time, and then afterwards I just felt … at peace." Jules huffed a laugh. "That probably sounds weirder – or more morbid – than it should."

"No, it doesn't."

"You did that for me, Leonard."

"I'm glad." A small smile glinted. But when Jules turned to head into the coffee shop, Leonard remained where he was. "Jules, may I ask you something, then?"

"Of course," Jules said, returning to face the man. Steeling himself to refuse Leonard if necessary.

"Last Wednesday, I couldn't help but notice you didn't tell your family about the arrest, though I'd only just told you. Even with the boiler breaking down, the arrest must have been on your mind."

"Yeah," he admitted.

"Perhaps you told them after I'd left."

"No, sorry."

Leonard took a moment, and even though it was chilly outside and getting dark already, he wouldn't let this go. "I don't presume to know you, Jules, but you don't seem the sort of person who'd keep secrets from his family. Do you feel you're protecting them?"

"Heavens, no." Jules guffawed. "If anything, I'd be protecting myself from being seen as the utter idiot I am."

Leonard was nodding. "Too much of this sort of crime goes unreported because people feel ashamed of being gulled. But then *you* reported it, Jules."

"Yes. Okay. Look, I think it's just what I said before. It's out of my hands now. I trust you to do your job – and obviously you *are* doing it, and very well indeed – and now it has very little to do with me. That's all."

"I see."

"Nothing more sinister than that, I promise." (And anyway, Jules thought, Ewan Byge.)

Leonard smiled at him, with a proper smile. He gestured towards the front door of Mr Oakley's. "Do you still have time for a coffee, Jules?"

"Of course," he said, though the evening was already starting to get away from him. "Thank you," Jules added as he swept through the door that Leonard held open for him.

"Hello, Jules," Daniel called over. "Hello, Jules' friend. You're late!"

Leonard solemnly replied, "Hello, Daniel, and that's entirely my fault, I'm afraid."

"Never mind, you're here now."

"Yes, never mind," Jules echoed. And he found himself reaching for Leonard's forearm, which felt strong and sinewy even under layers of shirt and jumper and coat – and Jules patted it reassuringly.

Leonard just smiled.

Ewan had called to ask Jules to come over again on that Saturday. "Talk me through this spreadsheet again," he'd said. Jules didn't hold out much hope for Ewan finally taking it on board, even though Ewan had added winningly, "Third time is the charm!"

If Jules had thought any more of his own charms, he might have hoped it was just an excuse to see him. Ewan surprised him, though, by being quieter and far more focused that day. They sat there together at the table with their coffee. Before, Ewan had always angled his chair away, twisting sideways to see the laptop, always ready to leap to his feet and escape. This time, he sat with his legs in under the table, and he paid attention. Mostly. It was apparent that he drifted off in thought occasionally, but mostly he watched and listened.

A possible explanation surfaced at last. "I'm heading home tomorrow," Ewan said, out of the blue.

"Your proper home."

"Yes, in Surrey."

Jules nodded, not betraying by a twitch or a wink that he'd already seen and memorised Ewan Byge's home address. He hadn't been looking, but when dealing with the man's paperwork – with his full permission, Jules might add – there were inevitably secrets revealed. Jules had already promised himself never to do anything untoward, or even anything at all, with such information.

"So I won't see you again for a while," Ewan continued. "But of course we'll be in touch. Phone and email." A pause grew significant before Ewan finally asked, "I should call you via the office … ?"

Jules huffed a bit, and shifted restlessly on the chair. "Could give you my direct number. If you want."

"I want." Ewan snagged his phone, called up the New Contact page, and handed it over. Moments later, he had Jules' first name, last name, company name, work number, mobile number, and birthday. Ewan didn't check out the details, but he put his phone aside with a chuckle, and remarked, "You'll soon be tired of hearing from me!"

"Somehow I doubt it," Jules lightly replied.

"The thing is … I've done all I needed to do up here."

Jules kept his gaze strictly focused on the laptop, telling himself he was imagining the slight wistfulness in Ewan's tone, the slight significance in his glance. Wishful thinking, that's all it was.

"And you'll be fine," Jules said, "getting your October accounts together on your own."

Ewan made a slightly doubtful 'um …' sound.

Jules threw him a glance. "I suspect you understand more about this than you think you do."

"Maybe," Ewan admitted. "Maybe a little more …"

"You just need to concentrate! Take it one step at a time, and concentrate."

"I'm sure …"

"How do you write your way through a whole damned novel, after all?"

Ewan grinned at him, and his beautiful sea-green eyes glinted with humour. "I take it one step at a time, and I concentrate."

"There you go."

They sat for a long quiet minute or two, close together and yet oddly far apart. Ewan had his head down, kind of like Leonard in Pondering Mode, except Ewan's fall of fine brown hair hid his profile. There certainly wasn't a moment in which Jules might lean into Ewan's orbit and let gravity do the rest ...

Jules let out the slightest of sighs, and began gathering his stuff together. "There you go," he murmured again, about thirty-nine times more wistful than he'd ever felt before. He stood, and went to shrug into his coat.

Ewan had followed him, trailing along behind. "Jules," he said, kind of haplessly.

And it wasn't enough. It just wasn't enough. They'd both been toying with the idea of something happening between them. Just a little something. Jules didn't fool himself about what it meant right now, even if he still harboured sweet dreams about what it might become. But the point was that saying goodbye – without one kiss – wasn't enough for either of them. Which was just the most fantastic thing ever.

Jules turned.

Ewan was *right there*, with his hands in his jeans pockets and his head down, his shaggy hair only adding to the general moroseness.

Except that Jules turned – and Ewan looked up with a spark in his eyes, half surprise and half hope – "All right?" Jules asked, already reaching for him – Ewan nodded –

And Jules reached both hands to cup that lovely face, and he leaned in to press a ravenous kiss to Ewan's mouth. He hardly gave the man time to respond before his hands were tracking down to Ewan's shoulders, and he swung them around and pushed Ewan back against the wall, Jules' lips trailing down Ewan's throat, his hands roughly exploring Ewan's chest before he crouched a little to mouth at a nipple through the cotton of Ewan's t-shirt. Ewan's breath snagged on a moan, and his hands came up to offer a caress of Jules' hair, his arms.

But by then Jules' hands had reached Ewan's hips, and he grasped them, revelling in it. Ewan let out a hoarse gasp, and squared his shoulders against the wall in order to push his nethers into Jules' embrace. It was perfectly obvious he was hard. Jules dropped to his knees, and looked up to ask permission. Ewan nodded again. "Yes." Jules simply leaned in and mouthed roughly at Ewan's cock through layers of denim and cotton. The groan that forced from Ewan's lips was the sweetest music Jules had ever heard.

It wouldn't take much. And there was no point in pretending this was anything other than quick and dirty. Jules slowly yet deliberately drove Ewan wild with hands and mouth, before at last undoing those jeans, and pushing them down just far enough. Ewan's gorgeous cock stood proud from a light dusting of hazel-brown hair. Jules knelt there staring at it for long moments, worshipping it, while his hand slipped within the denim to feel the intimate dip between hip and thigh.

"Jules," Ewan pleaded, his hands hovering as if wary of alighting on Jules and scaring him away.

Jules rasped his way up that silken skin with his tongue, and then he took the head into his mouth, and sucked and lapped and gentled and sucked some more. His hands ran up Ewan's stomach and chest, and his fingers rubbed at Ewan's nipples. It was all so much. So very much.

"Jules!" Ewan grabbed him by the arms now, brought him upright again for a kiss, the sweetest kiss, while Jules' hands swept back down to grasp Ewan and chase him to the finish line – and Ewan cried out, and Jules' mouth caught the sound so that it resonated within him, and Jules' hands were careful to catch every last dash of come –

Moments later Ewan was watching him with those sea-green eyes misty, while Jules licked all the salty goodness from his own hands.

By the time he was finished, Ewan was smiling again – almost as broadly as Jules was smiling on the inside – and Ewan's eyes were glinting in amusement. The mist had passed, and the sun was sparking off the ocean wave. Jules wiggled the tip of his tongue into the fork between two fingers, and he was done.

"Well," said Ewan.

Jules arched his brows. "Mmm?"

"That sure beats asking for an autograph."

"Oh!" Jules pealed as if Ewan was being outrageously amusing. Which he was, Jules supposed. Except Jules hardly knew how to react.

Ewan shifted his weight off the wall and onto his own two feet again, stuffing his hands into his jeans pockets. "Dear Jules," he said – though it sounded rather more bemused than affectionate, as if Ewan didn't quite know how to react either.

Jules had the answer for that. "Dear Ewan!" he countered, gathering up his things in a bright brisk fashion. He figured he'd better play it cool –

though God only knew how very much Jules wanted Ewan to be his very own HEA.

"What am I going to do with you?"

Heavens! Jules could give him a whole list. Apparently it wasn't wanted. "Uh … I suppose if you don't already know the answer to that, there's no point in me telling you."

"Do you really have to go?" Ewan pleaded … but he almost sounded relieved.

Jules put on his best wicked smile, and stage-whispered, "Always leave them wanting more."

"Oh, but I do, darling, I do!"

And Jules was out of there – out of the door and escaping down the stairs with a last flurry of a farewell wave. Then he was out on the pavement, and heading back towards the Tube station at a fast pace, his thoughts scattering like the last of the autumn leaves.

Talk about *Desire and Discombobulation*! Jules had always considered that rather a fanciful title. Until now.

It didn't take too long for Jules to decide to be pleased with himself. Any other response, whether ecstatic or miserable, might tempt madness.

He waited for a moment that evening in which he was alone with Jem. She was sitting comfortably slumped on the sofa, flipping through one of her magazines. Jules slid down to slump beside her, with his head on her shoulder.

Eventually, when she was done reading whatever the current article was, she asked, "What's up, Jules babe?"

"You know I was at Ewan's this morning?"

"Like we'd be allowed to forget."

"I, uh – I gave him a blow job."

Jem put her head back so she could examine Jules' silly face, which was no doubt betraying the whole wonderful (or was that woeful?) story.

"Huh," said Jem at last. "And what did he do?"

"He let me," Jules replied with great satisfaction.

"How very obliging of him!"

"I know, right?"

Jem tsk'd and shook her head, and lifted her magazine again. "Suppose you want congratulating," she said. After a sigh she offered, "Congrats, mate."

"Thanks, Gemstone!" he cried, completely ignoring her grudging tone, and leaning in further to press a kiss to her cheek.

She tsk'd again, but it was fonder this time. Quite a bit fonder.

nine

It seemed that Leonard was absolutely determined to do this paint job as thoroughly and professionally as he could. They'd planned it for a weekend on which he could devote both days to the task, so that they'd be doing the prep work on the Saturday, and the painting on the Sunday. It had become this Whole Big Thing.

"The rest of the house is going to look *so* shabby," Jules complained on the Friday evening as he, Archie and Jem sat around the table after dinner.

"I can't say that I mind very much," Archie retorted, with a very rare smug smile. "Anyway," he added, more like his usual cheerful self, "maybe it will inspire us to do the rest of the place, room by room."

"Maybe it will," Jules agreed.

"There's no reason we have to do it all at once. We could spread it out over a year or more."

Jem was sitting there looking very pleased with them all. "My little homemakers! Don't forget the master plan, though."

"As if you'd let us!" Jules protested.

"We're just getting into practice," Archie added. "Anyway, I've been feeling rather fond of this place. What if it became ours, eventually?"

"Fucked-up boiler and all?" Jules asked. "If we're scraping all our pennies together for a mortgage, we'll never afford a new one."

"We'd find a way, son."

"I suppose ..."

A moment later, Archie stood, and started clearing the plates. "I'm going to get these washed up, and then I thought I'd make it an early night. It's going to be a full weekend!" And Archie sounded as if he relished the prospect.

Jules could hardly help smile in response.

Leonard was due to arrive at nine on the Saturday morning, and of course he was there ringing the doorbell on the dot thereof. Jules almost danced down the stairs, and flung open the door. "Hellooooo!" he sang. "Come on in!"

Leonard smiled at him, and stepped inside. "Hello, Jules." He was carrying a battered old leather holdall, which he carefully put down on the wooden floorboards rather than on the rug. "How are you today?"

"Fighting fit and raring to go!"

That drew an appreciative glance from Leonard – and now that Leonard had stripped down to jeans, work boots and t-shirt, Jules found himself returning said appreciation. The elegant curve of his biceps disappearing up under those short sleeves was very enticing …

Jules shook himself. It wasn't fair to flirt. "Shall we head downstairs?" he asked Leonard. "Jem," he called back towards the kitchen, "make us some tea, would you?" Then he belatedly thought to check with Leonard, "Unless you'd prefer coffee?"

Leonard seemed amused by all this. "Tea would be very welcome, thank you, Jules. Milk and sugar, if I may."

"Of course. Jem!" he hollered. "Tea, please, and you remember how he likes it!"

"Kettle's on!" she called back. "Know about the tea. You can tell me the rest later!"

Jules opened his mouth to retort, but he was ashamed to find he had nothing. "Come on," he said to Leonard with a shrug, and they jogged downstairs in perfect synchronicity.

Archie was down there, tidying a few last things out of the way. He greeted Leonard warmly – then looked him over and added, "Those are very smart jeans, son. I wouldn't want them ruined."

'Son!' Jules silently protested. As far as he knew, that was the first time Archie had ever called anyone but Jules 'son', and that meant Archie was assuming way too much about Leonard and Jules. But Jules tried not to convey his discomfort, because Leonard was looking rather pleased by the attention.

"Thank you, Archie. They were a treat to myself."

"Very smart indeed," Archie repeated approvingly. "Well chosen."

Jules himself was dressed in the baggiest old grey sweatpants he owned, and a pink t-shirt that was so old and worn that it actually had little holes in the thin fabric under his arms. Which, now he thought about it, was really gross, and why on earth was he wearing it when they had company?

"Do you need something to change into?" Archie asked, already turning with an enquiring expression towards Jules.

"No – thank you for the thought, Archie, but I brought overalls." Leonard put his holdall down again, and crouched for a moment before drawing out a pair of paint-spotted white overalls. He shook them out and climbed into them, twisting and shrugging to get into the top half, with that wiry, flexible body of his.

Jules found himself mourning the disappearance of those sweetly curved biceps into the long sleeves – and then shook himself, having realised he was staring. "Um … What do we do first?"

Archie was smiling wryly at Jules, having caught him watching their companion. "We'll let Leonard call the shots, shall we?"

"Sure." It wasn't like Jules knew much about any of this, and he was probably totally wrong about the things he thought were obvious. He turned back to Leonard, who was looking around with an assessing eye, apparently working through a mental checklist with a little nod every now and then.

Archie had already put away everything he could, and moved a few easy items such as his table lamp up to the living room. He'd also spread an old tarpaulin over the three-quarter bed. "We're already well ahead," Leonard announced, "thanks to Archie. Our next task, Jules, is to move the furniture away from the walls, at least far enough to give us good access, and take down the curtains."

"I can help with that, too," Archie offered.

"He's probably stronger than me, and all," Jules added.

"Very well. After that, we'll need to share out the tasks. One of us can be filling in any cracks and gaps, another can be cleaning places that are usually hidden by bookcases and what-have-you, and the third can start running tape around the edges and protecting what needs it with old newspaper. Does any of that appeal?"

He was asking Jules what he most wanted to do. Jules was all too aware that his stupid pale cheeks were blushing in mortification. He was sure that Leonard must be the sort of person who regularly vacuumed behind bookcases, and by now Jules should be used to never quite making the grade. "Um … sounds like you should do the filling in, Leonard, and I'd better do the cleaning. If you're okay to start the taping, Dad?"

"Suits me," Archie confirmed.

"Good," said Leonard.

Jem had arrived in the middle of all that with a tray bearing four steaming mugs, so they all paused for a few long quiet moments to down their tea. Jules tuned the radio to Magic, on the grounds that the station's playlist would best cater for the differing ages and personalities of the four workers. And then they got on with it.

Jem single-handedly improved the light in the basement room by grubbing out the window well at the front of the house, and cleaning the windows both front and back. The others worked diligently on, knowing that their part of the transformation would happen the next day.

Between them, they'd chosen a paint colour called Lemon Spritz, which was a yellow so pale as to be almost white. They'd agreed it would make the most of the light, while adding a cheery warmth to the room.

Jules put together a tray of sandwiches and fruit for lunch, and they all sat around quietly for a while, resting and listening to the music. Then they got on with it again.

And they weren't quite finished by the time that Jules had to head upstairs to start cooking dinner. To be honest, he'd thought Leonard had been milking it to insist on taking two days to paint the room. But they were all people who liked to do things properly, and at this point it was actually seeming like a very good call.

Leonard had asked for steak and kidney pie for dinner. Jules had already cooked the meat and made the pastry the day before. He now needed to assemble and bake the pie, and then do the mashed potato and vegetables. Jem arrived once he was well underway; she lay the table for four, and fetched the spare chair.

"Should go sneak a look at your man," she whispered eventually.

"He's not my – anything," he hissed back.

"Go look at your Dad, then!"

Jules sighed, and put down the tea towel. He could hear that the telly was on quietly, so he didn't bother tiptoeing or anything, but he took care to only peer around the dividing wall. Archie had nodded off and was gently snuffling – with his head resting on a cushion that was on Leonard's shoulder. Meanwhile, Leonard sat there stoically watching *Strictly Come*

Dancing, whether he liked it or not, hardly even stirring to take a proper breath.

After a moment, Jules crept back to the kitchen. "Okay, points to Hufflepuff for adorableness," he grudgingly allowed.

Jem snorted into laughter. "You've already thought enough about him to sort him!"

"Oh. Well. Maybe I was talking about Dad."

Jem's laughter softened. "They're both Hufflepuff, aren't they? Just and loyal, patient and true." After a moment, she added, "I saw him putting that cushion under Archie's head. He was sooo gentle."

Jules fussed about with the cooking for a few moments, checking that the spuds were almost done, and then putting the greens and carrots on to steam. There was extra gravy left over from preparing the meat for the pie, which he'd heat in the microwave and have available on the table.

"Look," Jules eventually said. "It's not that Leonard isn't a nice bloke. It's just that …" He cast an imploring look at Jem, desperate for her understanding. "It's just that Ewan Byge let me give him a blow job a week ago. He's gone back home to Surrey for now, but … he'll be back. And he's … he's about the most incredible person I've ever met. It might seem like nothing much at the moment, but you can't expect me not to hope that 'nothing much' might become … something. Something real."

Jem was just standing there considering him coolly with her arms crossed. After a while she asked, "What house would you sort Ewan Byge into?"

"Ravenclaw, of course, for his clever mind."

This received a sceptical response from Jem – whom Jules had also sorted into Ravenclaw, though with Slytherin Rising. "Jules, do yourself a favour, and you think about that real carefully next time you see him, all right?"

Jules shrugged irritably. "All right! Heavens," he grumbled. "I wish you'd go back to being my friend. Sisters can be the most annoying creatures!"

"But we're all better off this way."

"Huh." He lifted his chin towards the living room. "Can you go wake Dad up? I'll be ready to start serving in a minute."

Jules had bought Guinness to drink with their dinner, and some had gone into the gravy, so they were all suitably mellow by the time they were done.

Leonard, in particular, sat there with a look of supreme contentment welling out of him. Archie chuckled, and asked, "As good as your mother's?"

Leonard took a moment to reconnect. Then he smiled at Archie, and dared to look at Jules. "I don't mean to be disloyal, but … even better."

Jules couldn't help but smile at the compliment, though he shrugged it off bashfully, uncomfortably. He got up to start collecting the plates, and Jem stood to help him.

"She never cooks any more," Leonard continued. "She still has her own flat – it's part of an independent living community – but the kitchen is hardly large enough to make a cup of tea in, and it's easier to let the canteen do the work when it comes to meals, of course."

"Is she nearby?" Archie asked.

"No, I'm afraid not. She and my father moved to Boscombe – near Bournemouth – when he retired. When he died, she wanted to stay on. It's a lovely place, very close to the sea, and she has her friends, her interests. I get down there about once a month." Leonard looked a little self-conscious. "That probably doesn't seem like much to a family such as yours, who still live together, but almost everyone in my family seems to like going their own way."

"And why not?" Archie asked rhetorically. "Interdependence comes in all forms, and if it doesn't suit you to live in each other's pockets, then why should you pretend otherwise?"

Leonard looked gratefully at Archie.

"And Boscombe has that marvellous beach," Archie continued, "and a pier, and views of the Isle of Wight."

"She really *didn't* want to come back to London."

"Who could blame her?" After a moment, Archie said, "I work in a care home, and contrary to popular opinion, a large portion of our residents are perfectly happy."

"I'm sure they are," Leonard agreed.

"Yeah, with *you* to look after them, Dad," Jules chipped in. He put his Good Host Hat on. "Anyone need anything? No? Shall we take a short break before pudding, then?"

"Yes," said Archie. "Give us a chance to do it full justice, son."

"Thank you, Jules," said Leonard. "That really was an excellent pie."

He tried not to squirm in embarrassment. "Well, thank you for helping

86

with the painting!"

"It's true, Jules babe," said Jem. "You outdid yourself." She didn't say, 'and for Leonard's sake, too,' but he heard it.

A change of subject was called for. Jules tugged on his Host Hat a bit tighter, and said, "Right. Let's play a little game. I want each of you to tell us The Funniest Thing you've ever heard."

Archie chuckled in anticipation, and Jem rolled her eyes, though she also sat up a little as if preparing to pay full attention. "You go first, son," said Archie.

They didn't play this very often, but Jules tried to go with something different each time. He dug back into old memories for this one. "Do you remember the Dame Edna Everage show when she interviewed Jane Seymour? Dame Edna started a question by saying to Jane, 'You've had three successful marriages ...'"

Jules' audience took a moment and then cracked up, just as Dame Edna's had done. Even Jane Seymour had laughed in appreciation of the observation. And Jules thought it hilarious, though he felt that Dame Edna made a fair point.

"Oh, Ginger Nut," said Jem, "that's so you. You are *such* a romantic."

"Is that your Funniest Thing?" Archie asked her. "Are you being Captain Obvious for a laugh?"

"Nah ..." Jem made a noble effort to quit chuckling, and said, "Okay, mine is: A Jew, a Christian, a Muslim and an atheist walk into a bar – and they sit down together and talk, and become friends, and they drink orange juice because they respect the Muslim's choices."

Again, after a moment, they all laughed. Jules added to the story: "And they lived Happily Ever After. The End."

Once they'd quietened, Archie had his turn. "The problem with kleptomaniacs is that they always take things literally."

More laughter. It was good for the soul. Jules sat there feeling it in his smile muscles and his stomach muscles, as if they'd been as well exercised that day as his arms and legs.

After a short while, Leonard said rather tentatively, "I don't suppose this will make you laugh, but I could tell you my favourite line from a novel."

"Yes, please," said Archie.

"Go on, then," said Jem.

Jules was silent, but when Leonard looked at him he nodded encouragingly.

"Speaking of Romantics with a capital R, this is from a satire called *Nightmare Abbey* by Thomas Love Peacock." Leonard sat a little more upright, not that he wasn't already, and declaimed with perfect enunciation, "'In the meantime, he drank Madeira, and laid deep schemes for a thorough repair of the crazy fabric of human nature.'"

They all stared at him for a long moment, before offering various huffs of appreciation.

"You're a real Don Quixote, aren't you, Leonard?" Jem observed.

Archie reached over to clap him on the shoulder. "Good for you, son. There's nothing quite as good as a dry humour."

'Son!' Jules silently protested again. But he smiled when Leonard looked at him, and then Jules stood. "Must be time for pudding!"

Again, it had been Leonard's choice, and he'd asked for treacle tart and custard – all of which Jules had made from scratch, of course. They all tucked in eagerly, making appreciative noises in Jules' direction.

When they finally sat back replete, Jem said, "Leonard, tonight's menu was your idea, wasn't it?"

"All the credit must go to the cook, though," Leonard promptly replied.

"Yeah, Jules did us proud. But *you*, Leonard, are a person of great taste and discernment."

Leonard was too polite to literally shrug this off, but he dissembled in a murmur, and put his head down. Which even Jules thought was a pity, despite the fact that he suspected Jem was referring to Leonard's taste for Jules, in which case he wanted to avoid the whole thing.

Oh, this was getting all too tricksy and tedious, when really what Jules cared about was just getting through until Ewan came back to town. Jules sighed. These days he wasn't even reading anything that wasn't written by Ewan. Jules knew he had it bad.

Jem's phone chimed to announce a message, and no one protested when she picked it up. "Ooh … speaking of people with great taste …"

Jules groaned. "For heaven's sake, you're not taking a booty call, are you?"

"Jealousy's a curse, Ginger Man."

"Misanthropy's worse."

She goggled her eyes at him, which was excessively annoying.

"Misanthropy? Where'd that come from?"

Jules mentally flailed for an explanation of this inexplicable thing he'd blurted. "Um … Because liking too many people too much ends up being just the same as liking nobody at all. Or even disliking everyone." There. That even made sense. Of a kind.

"Oh, Jules honey, it's not like that for me. Thought you got that." She sighed, and looked around the table at them each. And then she grinned. "For starters, I like you three just as much as you deserve. Which is quite a lot."

Archie smiled – but Leonard blanched under his olive skin.

Jem laughed. "Don't worry, Leonard. You're off my radar. And so is Jules. Gay men are the only ones safe from my predatory ways," she explained with a mock hushed tone as if she were narrating a nature program. "Unless they want to experiment, of course. A lot of them do. You might be surprised!"

"*I* never wanted to," Jules asserted. "Stephen Fry never wanted to."

"True," Jem agreed.

A silent moment drifted by, in which an awkward Leonard kept his head down but could be seen to glance in Archie's general direction.

"Yeah," said Jem. "Archie's straight. And you're wondering if he ever pinged my radar."

"Of course not!" Leonard protested – while Jules groaned, "Oh, please never use that metaphor again. That is absolutely *abominable*."

"Well, he did," Jem sailed remorselessly on. "And I propositioned him. But I was young. I didn't know any better. And of course he turned me down, as gently as a gentleman should."

Archie gallantly said, "I took it as a great compliment."

Jules added in sour tones, "Yeah, she's very free with the compliments."

No one responded to that, and the silence threatened to become really uncomfortable. Archie was calmly letting it all wash over him, but Leonard had his head down, and Jules thought he'd better reassure the man. "I'm sorry if this is all too much, Leonard," Jules offered. "Dad always encouraged us to be open and honest about who we are, what with me being gay, and Jem being … totally undefinable. So our conversations probably cross a few lines compared with most families."

"Love and sex are a part of life," Archie said in easy tones, "and a blessing to be respected and cherished. We have no need for secrets here."

Jules was watching Leonard, and he noticed the mental click once Archie mentioned secrets. Adding that to what Jules had already said to him about Jem's family imploding, meant that surely Leonard understood enough now about that whole sorry story. Nothing more would need explaining.

Leonard quietly said, "I think that's a truly admirable creed to teach your children, Mr Madigan."

"Thank you, son." Another moment passed, a whole lot more comfortable now. And then Archie stood. "Right! Let's get this all cleaned away. That was a marvellous dinner, Jules, and you really did do us proud."

It was getting late, and soon the Tube would stop running. Jules was vaguely aware that Leonard had disappeared to use the facilities, and had then headed for his gear. He was taking his time to put on his coat and otherwise get organised.

Jules found himself beset by family. Archie was looking worried, which made Jules' heart sink before he even knew what the problem was. "Leonard's leaving," Archie whispered.

"You should ask him to stay," Jem hissed. "It's not like you don't have a double bed."

Jules gaped at her, overacting like a silent movie star. "What, now you want me to put out in return for him painting Dad's room?!"

"No, you idiot. You wouldn't have to *do* anything."

Jules shrugged this off uncomfortably, and then wriggled like his skin was crawling.

"No, Jules is right," Archie put in.

"*Thank you*, Dad."

"It wouldn't be fair on Leonard."

"What?!"

"Poor man," Archie muttered.

Jules groaned, and decided he really didn't want to hear any more along those lines. On the other hand, he did have to admit that it wasn't fair on Leonard to travel alone on a cold night to the section house, and then be expected to commute back again on a Sunday morning. "All right. I'll go ask him to stay." Something told him that neither Archie nor Jem would make the offer if Jules didn't. He didn't know whether that was reassuring or not.

"If anyone's sharing, though, it's Dad in with me."

Archie nodded immediately, as if that was perfectly acceptable.

"All right," Jules repeated. And he took a breath, and headed for the hallway.

Leonard took one look at him, and shrugged on his coat. "I'd better be –"

"Stay," said Jules. "You'd better stay for the night. It makes no sense to go. The only question is," he carried on, "*where* will you stay?"

Leonard's head was down, but he seemed to turn a bit pink if the tips of his ears were anything to go by. He didn't venture any thoughts on The Bed Situation, though.

"We have a sofa bed in the living room, but Dad's sleeping there. He didn't want to be downstairs with everything a mess and no curtains on the windows tonight – or with the paint smell tomorrow, of course. But I guess Dad can share with me, and you can –"

"Oh, no," Leonard said, interrupting for maybe the first time ever. He was usually too polite to talk over anyone. "I'd be happy to sleep downstairs in Archie's bed, if he wouldn't mind."

"With the morning light and the chaos?"

"I'm sure it will be nothing compared to the section house. You get used to sleeping through all kinds of disruptions there."

"Oh," said Jules. Would it be as easy as that? He turned towards where he knew the others were waiting just out of sight. "Dad, Leonard says he'll have your bed in the basement, if you don't mind."

Archie made an appearance. "That would be absolutely fine. Thank you, Leonard."

"No, it's me who should be thanking you."

Jules interrupted the Love Fest. "One more question, then, Leonard. What do you like for breakfast?"

"I'll be happy with whatever you're having, Jules."

He grinned at the not unexpected response. "No, come on. I said I'd cook your favourite things this weekend, and I meant it."

Leonard was definitely a bit pink by now. But he dared to ask for, "Pancakes, then?"

"Pancakes, it is." Jules gestured back towards Archie and Jem. "I think we're all about to turn in, so …"

"Of course," said Leonard. He took his coat and scarf off, then added,

"I left my bag downstairs, so I'll just go get organised."

"Sure." Jules took a step or two, intending to follow him down and help clear the bed.

They were followed by calls of "Goodnight, Leonard!" and "Thank you for all you've done today!"

"Goodnight!" Leonard called back. "It's been a pleasure." And then he was heading downstairs, with Jules just behind him.

They cleared the gear and the tarpaulin off the bed, and Jules straightened it up a bit. Then he stood with his hands in his pockets, and his gaze anywhere that Leonard's wasn't – before realising there was more to do. He headed for where the old chest of drawers stood askew, a few feet away from the wall. "The beds were changed during the week, but there's clean sheets in the bottom drawer here. I'll help you with them."

"No, I'm sure it will be fine, Jules. It's only for one night."

For a moment, Jules thought about insisting, but then let his Scrupulous Host instincts be overridden. "Well, I'll put a fresh towel in the bathroom for you anyway," Jules said. "Is there anything else you need?"

"No, thank you, Jules. Really, I'll be fine."

Jules lingered despite himself. He really didn't want to ask whether Leonard had brought a spare pair of underwear, and he certainly didn't want to offer a pair of his own, but common decency made him feel like a cowardly loser.

After a few moments, though, Leonard took pity on him. He lifted his (rather large) holdall, and put it on a tarp-covered chair, saying with a small smile, "I packed for all foreseeable eventualities."

"Good to know. We'll be all set to deal with the zombie apocalypse, then?"

"I'm always prepared for that."

"Excellent." Jules offered the man a wry smile, and turned to head for the stairs. "Goodnight, then."

"Goodnight," Leonard replied. But then he said, "Jules –"

"Yes?"

"Jules, may I ask you something? A personal question," Leonard added, darting a glance towards the stairs, no doubt indicating that he didn't want to be overheard by Archie.

"Sure," said Jules. His heart was sinking, just a little, but he headed back closer to Leonard so they could talk with lowered voices.

Leonard sat down on the side of the bed, leaving plenty of room – and after a moment Jules took the hint and sat down as well, not within reach but not too far away from the man either. "Jules, I was wondering about your mother. You can tell me to mind my own business, of course, but it occurred to me that I hadn't seen one photo of her, either down here or in the living room, or anywhere else in the house. I was just … surprised. Curious, and surprised."

Jules nodded, and thought about what to say. It had been such a long time since anyone had asked, though he was sure that people made their own assumptions. If it even occurred to them. Well, he might as well just tell the story without sugar-coating. No doubt Leonard had heard much worse. "She left us," said Jules. "Back when I was a little kid. I hardly even remember her."

"She *left* you?"

"Yes."

"She left you." Apparently Leonard could hardly even get his head around that. "I'm sorry, I had assumed she'd died."

"There's no need to be sorry."

Leonard was still boggling. He turned to look directly at Jules, and asked, "Why on earth would anyone leave your father?"

Jules huffed a laugh. "I know, right? Dad said she was just one of those people who always think the grass is greener somewhere else. Jem used to call her The Bolter. But I don't know how she managed to leave Dad. It was the hardest thing I ever did, moving here from Essex without him. You probably realise how happy I was when Dad ended up deciding to come, too."

"I can guess. He really is a wonderful person."

"He's been the best Dad, absolutely. He had to fight to keep custody of me, 'cause back then they didn't think much of single fathers. Not that my Mum wanted custody at all – she was already long gone – but there was a real chance they'd have put me in foster care. Thank God they didn't!"

"Indeed," Leonard murmured.

"And Dad proved himself soon enough, of course, so by the time Jem needed a new home – oh, years later – there were no questions at all about whether we were suitable. The only negative thing I ever heard said was that he's over-protective. But to be honest, that's something I've been glad of, and not just because I was growing up gay. I don't think any child has ever been loved as well as I have."

Leonard was just watching him with those lovely dark eyes and a beautifully empathic expression.

"We do have some photos of my Mum, in the family album. It's not like I have any bad memories of her. I think I was too young to even register she was gone, until a long time after. But will you understand," Jules asked Leonard, "if I say I was never interested in finding her again? A lot of people seemed to assume I'd want to 'reconcile' with her once I was older. I don't resent her or anything, and I hope she's happy and she found what she was looking for – but I've never felt the need for her to be part of my life. I'm fine with how things are."

"I understand," said Leonard, just very quietly and simply.

Jules smiled at him, and they sat there together for a long contemplative moment.

"My Mum is who I got my red hair and blindingly white skin from, of course. I'm jealous of you," Jules said, gesturing towards the lovely olive tones of Leonard's bare forearm. "I'm too pale at the best of times, but as soon as I'm the slightest bit tired or ill, I look like I should be in the morgue."

Leonard smiled a little uncomfortably, and had to look elsewhere. Eventually he said, "I suspect you're exaggerating for comic effect."

"I'm not, though. I just freckle and burn if I spend too long outside. Not an attractive look. I always thought of you as sun-kissed. Much preferable."

"Ah." Leonard peered down at his own skin as if considering it for the first time in a long while.

"So," Jules finally ventured, "can I ask you an inappropriate personal question?"

"Of course." That dark gaze swung back to fix on Jules. Apparently Leonard was ready to lay his whole life open to Jules' regard.

Which felt like a bit too much, but Jules decided to forge on anyway. "Do you spend a lot of time outdoors, then, or … ?"

"Both," Leonard replied to the spoken and unspoken parts of the question. "My duties only have me behind a desk about half the time. Especially now I'm living at the section house, where you're basically considered on call, day and night. Also, I run three or four times a week, if

I can get away."

"I knew it!" At Leonard's slightly puzzled glance, Jules elaborated in more reasonable tones, "Well, I guessed you were a runner. You've got that kind of build. Not like me! I know I'm a tad too cuddly. We're opposites in so many ways."

Leonard's head went down for a moment as he pondered that, and when he looked up again it seemed as if he wasn't sure whether it was a good thing or a bad thing that they had their differences.

"Anyway," Jules prompted, "you spend time outdoors, and … ?"

"Oh, yes." Leonard nodded. "I was given a head start by a Malaysian grandparent. My grandmother on my father's side. My grandfather met her while doing his National Service."

"Awesome! Is that the granddad who worked at your school?"

"Yes. I spent a fair amount of time with them while I was growing up. They were good people."

Jules was ambushed by a yawn, and belatedly remembered it was unfair to keep Leonard sitting up after such a long day. "There's an interesting story there, I'm sure, but I'd better not pester you for it now." Jules got up, and wandered a step or two towards the stairs. "I'll say goodnight, Leonard. I hope you sleep well!"

"You, too, Jules. Goodnight."

And Jules finally made his escape. He stepped lightly past a slumbering Archie in the living room, and then he headed upstairs to bed, turning off a last light or two as he went.

Once Jules was in his pyjamas he burrowed in alone under the duvet, and wrapped both arms around the spare pillow. He felt on edge, and tried to sooth himself by daydreaming in a scattered kind of way about Ewan, and about Dexter and Mike, and hardly thinking at all about Leonard.

He couldn't control his dreams, though.

The next morning, Jules took a mug of coffee down to Leonard – only to find that he was already awake and dressed, and sanding back some of the wall filler he'd applied. "You're up early," Jules said. "I hope you weren't too uncomfortable."

"Not at all. Thank you, Jules," Leonard added, taking the coffee gratefully. "I was very comfortable indeed, but unless I'm on shifts I'm afraid I'm always up early."

Jules nodded, and glanced around the room they'd soon be painting. It looked so much better already for their attentions, and no doubt it would be transformed by that evening. Still, first things first. "Come upstairs when you're ready. I'll start cooking the pancakes."

Leonard smiled. "Then I'll come up now."

The first mouthfuls of pancake were met with happy moans from all four of them – including the cook – and then everyone got on with the business of eating.

Finally, when they sat back feeling contentedly full, and Jules was thinking vaguely about the necessity of getting up to make a pot of coffee … Finally Leonard murmured, quietly as if he almost wasn't aware of saying anything out loud, "Oh, Jules. You know the way to a man's heart, all right."

A moment's startled silence.

And then Jem guffawed, and Archie laughed and reached to grasp Leonard by the shoulder. And Jules sighed, and stated collecting up the plates.

Late that evening, with Archie's room looking as fresh as a daisy, and all the paint brushes and rollers rinsed clean, it was finally time for Leonard to leave. Jules helped him pack up, and then stood outside the front door despite the evening air turning cool, watching Leonard walk off to the Tube station carrying his holdall. Leonard didn't look back, which was probably just as well.

Jem came to lean against the door jamb with her arms crossed. "You've found him, haven't you, Jules? You've found The One."

"Yeah." Jules shivered a little, and looked up into the cloudy night sky. "I found him when I met Ewan Byge."

"*Not* that idiot. You know I'm talking about Leonard."

Jules sighed. "Ah, but what would Police Constable Leonard Edgar want with a cuddly ginger guy, who couldn't act straight to save himself, who's gullible enough to be defrauded, and doesn't even think to paint his father's room?"

"Dunno, when you put it like that," she said. "But he sure wants something."

Jules was pleased to find, however, that Ewan Byge seemed to want something from Jules as well. Ewan called Jules on his mobile at about four-thirty on the Monday afternoon, and there was something wickedly flirtatious in the way he said, "Hello, Jules."

"Good afternoon, Mr Byge," Jules replied in faux professional tones. "How may I help you?"

Ewan chuckled. "You can start by telling me how you are. I hope you're well? How's your day been?"

"I *am* well, thank you, and my day's been fine – though it's all the better for hearing from you, of course."

"Of course!" Ewan left one of his Significant Pauses. "You're in the office, I suppose, and I shouldn't be wasting your time. But it didn't feel right to call you out of hours."

Jules immediately dropped the silly voice he'd put on. "Actually," he confessed, though it was all kinds of deliciously wrong – "I'm working from home today. Which means I'm in my usual Working from Home attire ... my pyjamas!"

Another gloriously wicked chuckle from Ewan – which was utterly delightful, of course, but Jules facepalmed. Honestly, could he *be* any more inappropriate?

"I'm sorry, I really shouldn't have told you that," Jules said.

"And I probably shouldn't tell you that I never wear pyjamas! I never wear anything at all in bed."

"Oh my ..." Jules murmured. Despite the cool autumn day, he was feeling distinctly warm. He tried to mentally string some words together along the lines of demanding proof of such an outrageous claim.

A long moment passed. "Well," Ewan eventually said. "That conversation just went from nought to sixty in five seconds flat! It seems a bit pointless to attempt small talk now."

"We could try talking about the Really Important Things. Like, you could tell me what you've been writing today."

"Oh …" Ewan laughed a little dryly. "I'm getting towards the end of my next book."

"A happy ending, of course?"

"Of course! Partly because I find the middle hardest to write. The second act is always a struggle. I'm even happier than the characters to reach the end, believe me!"

Which was certainly an interesting insight to ponder. "It doesn't show," Jules said. "I never would have guessed you struggle with writing any part of a book."

"Glad to hear it. I do put the work in, but I have to thank my editors, too. They're never slow to tell me when something isn't up to scratch."

"What's this one called? What's its title?"

"Ah …" Ewan laughed again, happier this time. "I'm not supposed to tell anyone!"

"Aw … That's okay. I understand."

"I'll tell *you*, though, Jules. If you promise not to Tweet about it or anything."

Jules let out something that might have been a squeak – though he blurted, "Of course I wouldn't, but you don't have to!"

"I know I can trust you. Okay, it's a follow-up to *Sherbet and Sin*, and it's called *Marriage and Marjoram*."

Jules giggled. "That's cool. I like these alliterative titles of yours."

"And I like a man who can use the word 'alliterative' in ordinary conversation."

He basked in that for a moment, and then said in a low, serious tone, "I like that you were so active for Marriage Equality, you know. I like it a lot."

"Well," said Ewan. "It was an important issue."

"Yes, it was. It still is."

"Yes." Another pause, which somehow felt tense, even over the phone. Finally Ewan said, "Jules. Are you on Tinder? Or Grindr?"

"What?" This time the noise Jules made was brittle. It was supposed to be a laugh. "Is this a booty call, Mr Byge?"

"Oh, my darling. If only I wasn't adrift in the wilds of Surrey! I'd be there like a shot."

It seemed that they both sighed over missed opportunities. Then Jules said, a tad defiantly, "I'm not, though. On those sites, I mean. I don't want to come across as a prude or anything, and it's not that I don't hook up when I want to … but I'm a romantic." He added, "Like you."

Ewan really did sigh then. "Like me, yeah." And he was hurriedly signing off. "Well, I've kept you on the line talking about nothing much for far too long. Thanks for indulging me! And on a work day, too. Catch you later, Jules."

"Catch you –" the connection went dead – "later, Ewan."

Jules carefully put the phone down, and frowned. He puzzled over the conversation for several minutes, replaying it in his head in the hopes he'd remember most of it. He had no idea what it was about, or what Ewan's motivation had been. But sometimes these early Getting to Know You days were like that … weren't they? It would all click at some stage, and then they'd be cruising along together at sixty miles per hour without a care in the world.

Ten

"The court hearing is on Friday," Leonard quietly announced over coffee on the Wednesday evening.

Jules actually had to think for a moment before realisation dawned. "The Bad Guy's court date? That's come around quickly."

Leonard frowned. "Do you think so? I think it's been unconscionably delayed. I understand he's still going to plead guilty, but I hope his lawyers aren't planning anything 'clever'."

Jules just nodded vaguely. It really didn't feel like the case had anything to do with him at all any more. He'd reported it and made his statement, and he was pretty sure he would never get his money back, so that was that. Wasn't it?

"I know it's short notice, and you'd need to take time off work, Jules, but would you come to court that day?"

"Me? Why? I thought you said I wouldn't have to give evidence?"

"No, you won't. But I thought you'd like to be there. You can watch him plead guilty, and then later in the day he'll be sentenced. I thought you'd like to hear that."

Jules boggled a bit, and tried to imagine himself there. Of course his only reference was crime dramas on the telly, which didn't exactly bode well. On the other hand, he had to assume that the drama was always overplayed compared to what it was like in Real Life. After a long moment Jules asked, "Will you be there?"

"If you are," Leonard replied. "Ordinarily I wouldn't, but of course I'll accompany you, if you want to attend."

"Oh," said Jules. "But what do you mean, ordinarily you wouldn't? It was your arrest!"

Leonard essayed a shrug. "Yes, but once the suspect has been charged, the CPS – the Crown Prosecution Service – takes over the case. Ordinarily, I wouldn't have anything more to do with it."

"But …" Jules ground to a halt. Something was very odd about all that, but he couldn't quite get his head around it. There was too much else going on as well.

A silence stretched. Their coffees were being ignored and going cold.

Leonard finally said, "Do you remember we talked about you making a victim personal statement?"

Jules probably looked as blank as he felt. "Not the witness statement?"

"No. This is the statement about how the offence has affected you. Not only the loss of money, but the loss of trust, the sense of hurt. These can be taken into account when sentencing."

"I remember," Jules said. He hadn't wanted to at the time, and the thought of doing it now or on Friday just made him feel anxious. Which was silly, wasn't it?

"Jules," said Leonard with his gentle tones fully deployed, "remember I said there were other people involved, other victims? Some of them have chosen to provide victim personal statements. I thought you might like to hear them being read out. That's all. I thought it might do you good."

"The thing is," said Jules, "I don't actually feel all that bad about it, not any more. I feel like an enormous fool, but maybe that was a lesson I needed to learn! I just don't think he should get away with taking advantage of fans, that's all. We're worth better than that."

Leonard smiled, and reached to let a fingertip brush briefly across the back of Jules' hand. "You're a good person, Jules Madigan."

"And anyway," Jules blabbed on now that he was into the swing of it, "I met you because of this. And I met Ewan. I mean, *really* met him, thanks to you. Not just as a fan, but as a potential friend."

Leonard was doing the Stoic Police Officer thing, which might mean that on the inside he was wincing just the slightest bit.

"Acquaintance, anyway," Jules finished a tad lamely.

"I'm very glad that you've got something good out of all this."

"Thanks to you!"

Leonard really did wince then.

They'd agreed to meet outside the court house on Marylebone Road. Jules hadn't realised how huge and daunting the building was – but of course Leonard, being his usual chivalrous self, was already there waiting despite Jules being totally punctual. "Hello, Jules," said Leonard, with that little smile of his that seemed to be full of delightful secrets. He was in his uniform, including the custodian helmet with the low brim that shielded his eyes. On anyone else it tended to look ridiculous, Jules thought, but Leonard was always dignified.

"Hello, Leonard," Jules replied, managing an edgy smile in return.

Leonard reached a hand as if intending to grasp Jules' shoulder, just as Archie sometimes did, but then let his hand fall away again mid-gesture. "There's nothing to be worried about."

"Well, no, I guess I …" Jules sighed. "I don't know. This is probably silly, but today the Bad Guy becomes flesh and blood for me, yeah?"

"Yes."

"You deal with them every day. It's not such a big deal for you."

"No, you're right." Leonard still seemed to be suppressing some marvellous secret. "I think you'll find it worthwhile, though."

"All right. Come on, then. Let's do this thing!"

They headed inside, Leonard taking off his helmet and tucking it in the crook of his arm. There were security barriers in place, of course. Leonard indicated a side gate. "I can go straight through – and if I asked them they'd probably let you through with me. But they shouldn't, so I'd rather not ask."

"No, of course. That's fine." Jules went through the rigmarole of his satchel being scanned, and of walking through the metal detector. It only took a few moments, and Leonard was there to meet him on the other side. Jules smiled at Leonard's apologetic look, and suppressed a quip. It didn't do to have a sense of humour in the vicinity of security these days.

"We have a little while to wait for our case, but I thought you'd like to sit in the courtroom. Get acclimatised, as it were."

"All right. Sure." They climbed an airy glass-and-steel staircase to the first floor.

"We're expected to be quiet while we're in there, but you can whisper to me if you have any questions."

Jules winked at the man.

The tips of Leonard's ears went pink. "Also, as soon as we're inside, we need to pause and bow to the magistrates before sitting down. A respectful nod will do."

"Seriously?" Jules couldn't remember seeing that on any TV shows. Of course people stood when a judge entered or left the room, but he couldn't remember anyone bowing.

"Yes. The practice actually originated as a recognition of the Royal Coat of Arms that you'll see on the wall behind the magistrates. But these days, it's probably more about the people and the role."

"Okay," Jules said with a smile. That almost sounded like fun. An antiquated ritual, no less.

So that's what they did, and one of the three magistrates beamed up at them with a fond twinkle in his eyes that must have been for Leonard. They were in a public gallery overlooking the courtroom proper. The audience was pretty sparse, so they had no problems finding a place to sit together up the back, behind the prosecution – which Jules was pleased to find had been correctly placed (on the groom's side, as it were) on all the TV shows he'd ever watched.

Jules just sat there taking it all in. The atmosphere was surprisingly relaxed and there was the oddly reassuring feeling that for almost everyone there this was just another ordinary day. Definitely less dramatic than on the telly.

People came and went, gathering at the defence and prosecution tables, and then scattering again with the bang of a gavel. No one – not even the magistrates – wore wigs, and only a couple of people wore black robes. They bustled around, making announcements, fetching people and handling files, with an occasional swish and billow of fabric. There wasn't a jury, of course. Jules had known enough to expect that, at least. Just the three magistrates.

Jules had relaxed into the rhythm of it when suddenly, at about midday, the Bad Guy's name was called.

Jules sat up, straight and tense. Leonard shifted a little closer. Not touching, but reminding Jules of his presence. Of the three people now gathered at the defence table, it was obvious who the Bad Guy was. Obvious which were the professionals and which the defendant, from his truculent attitude if nothing else. Jules found himself staring, hardly aware of the charges being read out – until his own name was mentioned and he belatedly realised that he was only one person in a not insignificant list of people who'd been defrauded in some way by this man. Of course Leonard had said he wasn't the only victim, but that hadn't felt real to Jules until now. He hadn't been the only idiot, the only one who'd wanted to believe. That counted.

"How do you plead?"

"Guilty."

Jules' heart thumped, and he cast a grateful look at Leonard. It mattered that the Bad Guy, no matter how grudgingly, admitted he knew he'd done Jules wrong. That counted, too.

It seemed clear from his scowl that the Bad Guy didn't like pleading guilty, but perhaps he realised he had little choice. No doubt there were a few things in that long list of charges that he'd like to argue about, but Jules suspected the sentencing would be a little more lenient if the defendant didn't waste any more of the court's time than was necessary.

"Very well," said the middle of the three magistrates. "We'll hear victim personal statements now."

First one victim and then a second came into court, were sworn in, and then stood in the witness box to read out their statements. They were people so different to Jules in so many ways, and yet also exactly the same. They described the initial thrill and then the growing suspicion and the disappointment of ordering memorabilia from this man. The hurt and humiliation of realising they'd been had. The inconvenience and the pain of losing a significant amount of dosh.

They were brave, getting up there not only in defiance of the Bad Guy but also in telling the other people in court – and at least potentially the whole world – of how foolish they'd been.

Jules was occasionally told he was brave. But he hadn't been brave enough to do this. And he was sorry for it now. One of the victims was barely more than a kid who'd lost three times as much as Jules had, on signed scripts and props from a sci-fi show. Gear that had, of course, never arrived. Jules watched his fellow fans with an aching heart.

And then … And then … And then Ewan Byge was ushered into the witness box.

Ewan seemed his usual comfortable, confident self, but he glanced around the courtroom as if needing to take it all in – and he looked up, and he happened to spy Jules, and Ewan broke into the widest, most gorgeous grin. Jules was grinning back like a mad thing, but he didn't mind when Ewan had to turn away and pay attention. Jules just stared and stared, drinking in the sight … Ewan wasn't in a suit, but he looked very smart in trousers, shirt and a fine-knit jumper. His hazel-brown hair shifted with every move and glinted like silk.

Ewan was sworn in with his hand on the Bible (though to be honest,

Jules didn't think he was at all religious), and then he was asked to read out his statement. And of course he was a writer, so he was far more eloquent than Jules could ever have been.

"I'm making this statement on behalf of myself and the other writers and creators whose names have been used in a fraud. And not only were our names used, but objects that matter to us, and details of our personal and professional lives as well. Though none of us were complicit in this crime, our names are tarnished by association. It is a hurtful thing to be used in such a way.

"That is a relatively small matter, however, compared to the hurt this man has caused our readers and viewers. He has taken callous advantage of their innocent enthusiasm for reading books, for watching television and films. He has abused their trust in the world, and tainted their associations with creations that they loved. They have lost money I'm sure none of them could afford. They paid quite exorbitant amounts to have a souvenir of something they deeply cared about in their lives. Only to be disappointed.

"I can't claim that only bad things have come from this, however, because as a result I've been privileged to meet and befriend a young man who loves my books. I write romances, and he brings his whole heart to the reading of them. It's unforgivable to even bruise such a soul, let alone cut him to the quick. And he's smart, too – an accountant, a real wiz with figures which are completely beyond me. But this whole affair has made him doubt his own judgement, and doubt the wisdom of his own trusting nature.

"His name is Jules Madigan. If he is speaking to you directly today (and actually I've since found out that he isn't), I suspect he'll be too modest to say the things I'm saying now. Jules is Good People. All the victims in this case are Good People. Your Worships, when you're sentencing this man who cruelly took advantage of Jules and these others, I hope that fact will remain clear in your mind's eye.

"Thank you."

For a moment, Jules was about to burst into rapturous applause – but the courtroom remained silent, of course, and he managed to restrain himself. Ewan looked up at Jules again and smiled, before stepping down from the witness box and disappearing back underneath the public gallery. Jules' hands were clasped together, and his heart was going thumperty-thump, thumperty-thump.

"Very well. We'll resume for sentencing at –"

"Three p.m., ma'am."

"Three p.m."

"All rise."

Everyone got to their feet, and the magistrates left via a door at the back of the courtroom.

Jules found himself standing there beside Leonard with the most awestruck look on his face, he just knew it.

Leonard smiled gently at him. "I guessed you would want to be here."

"You guessed right! Thank you." Jules beamed at the man. "Thank you. That was fantastic."

"Come on, then. I'm sure he's waiting outside for you."

Jules just shook his head, for once lost for words. Jittery, he followed Leonard out of the court and down to the large foyer – and there, as promised, was Ewan waiting with that beautiful grin on his face.

"Hello, Jules," said Ewan as they walked up to him.

"Oh My God, that was *fantastic*," was all that Jules could find to say. "Thank you so much!"

"You're welcome. Hey, this man hurts my brand, he hurts my fans, then my only problem is with him."

Leonard asked Ewan, "Are you going to stay for the sentencing?"

"Hell yes."

"Will you keep Jules company, then?"

"It would be my pleasure. There must be a café around here somewhere. We'll grab a sandwich and a coffee while we're waiting."

Leonard turned to Jules. "I'd better get back to work, I'm sorry. But I leave you in good hands."

Jules smiled at him. "Thank you again. Thanks for making sure I came. You were right, it helped a lot."

Leonard nodded in farewell, to Ewan, to Jules. He said, "Goodbye, Jules." And he turned and headed for the exit.

"See you, Leonard!" Jules called to his departing back. But then Ewan demanded a hundred and ten percent of his attention.

They ended up sitting at the outdoor tables of a pub near Marylebone

Station. It was a bright though chilly day, but they were both rugged up in coats and scarves, and Jules for one was feeling no pain. He was just sitting there across from Ewan Byge, glowing from the inside. He wasn't even hungry, but Ewan ordered a burger and a beer, and Jules said, "The same for me, thanks."

Ewan was leaning forward on the table, all animated chat about trying to finish his latest book, *Marriage and Marjoram*, the wild weather they'd been having in Surrey, his plans for his next novel, *Sensational* – "Dedicated to you, of course, Jules Madigan."

Jules blushed about as red as his hair, which he knew would not be a good look. But O-M-G a book dedicated to him? When he was nothing but a very ordinary accountant? It didn't bear thinking about.

When Ewan seemed to be winding down a bit, Jules took refuge in the mundane. "Are you keeping your October accounts up to date? Is it starting to make sense now?"

Ewan blessed him with an absurdly grateful smile. "You got me set up perfectly. Whenever I get in a muddle, I just look back at the previous months to see how you did things. Oh, but there was one thing I got stuck on. Which category do I put webhosting costs into? Is it 'Internet and Telephone' or 'Other Computer Costs'?"

"The Internet category," Jules promptly replied, "because it's about the cost of using the internet to host a website."

"What about when I buy a new font?"

"That's the Other Computer category, because it's equivalent to software."

Ewan was madly impressed. "You're brilliant, you are," he declared, with a grin that Jules would have given anything to see every day of his life.

"I'm nothing," Jules managed to say. His voice was probably as wobbly as his cheeks were blotchy. "Not anywhere near as brilliant as you. To be a writer – it must be the most marvellous thing."

"Well," said Ewan, in a moment of uncharacteristic humility, "it's not really so very special."

Jules gave a vehement shake of his head. "No. Words are powerful things. You persuaded people in that courtroom with your words. And you sure have an effect on me with your stories …"

"My romances," Ewan corrected him, with a self-conscious grimace.

"God, I am finding the last scene of this one hard to finish, though."

Jules puzzled over that for a moment, thinking back to other times they'd talked about Ewan's writing habits. "I thought you said – Didn't you say that it was the middles you struggled with?"

"I know, I know, and I do – but this one, with the *Marriage* title, has to have the full-blown wedding scene at the end. It's what people will expect."

"And that's not … fun? I would have thought that'd be terrific fun to write! Like, the wonderful thing about gay marriage is that we can take all the best bits of traditional weddings, and make the rest up to suit ourselves."

Ewan scrunched his face up, and said apologetically, "Jules, you are such a sweetheart, but I think you've got the wrong idea about me."

"Oh." Jules mulled over that one, clumsily scrambling for what he might have misunderstood.

Their burgers finally arrived, and they both sat there ignoring them, except for Ewan morosely eating a chip or two with his fingers.

Finally Jules asked very tentatively, "You're not really … gay?" And he would just die if Ewan answered that no, he wasn't. But surely, oh dear God, surely Ewan hadn't minded Jules pouncing on him that day …

"Oh," said Ewan. "Oh, well, I guess I'm a Kinsey 5 or thereabouts … Maybe even a 4 on a good day with fair winds and following seas."

"That's okay," Jules responded, because of course no one should feel bad about being who they were. Not when it came to sexuality, anyway. "I'm a Kinsey 6, but I shouldn't have assumed –"

Ewan interrupted him. "It's not that so much as …"

Jules had to prompt him to continue. "So much as what?"

"This whole gay marriage thing." Ewan had picked up another chip, but now tossed it back down onto his plate. "I'm *not* a romantic, Jules," he blurted out, suddenly piercing Jules through with that sharp green gaze. "I can't see me ever marrying. I like my independence too much!"

The earth shifted under Jules' feet. It seemed that everything he knew was wrong. "But the books you write –"

"I write about yachting, too, but I'm not into boats. I write about growing herbs, and believe me I do not have a green thumb, not at all."

"No, but I mean – You were such an advocate for Marriage Equality! You were so outspoken. You were our unofficial poster boy! I guess I just assumed that … you wanted it for yourself."

"Not so much. Not for me personally. It was a human rights issue, you see. It was about putting us on a more equal footing with the straights." Ewan leaned forward again, easily falling into the old arguments. "The family is the cornerstone of our society. The basic unit, and everything is organised around that. We all know how family was traditionally defined. And if we queers are excluded from that definition, then we're pushed right to the edge of our culture, or even outside it."

"A human rights issue," Jules echoed.

"Don't you agree?"

"You're not wrong. It is. Of course it is." He let out a laugh which no doubt conveyed his disillusionment. "You should meet my friend – my sister, Jem. You'd understand each other perfectly."

"Plus of course it was good for the branding. But if you can look past the Ewan Byge, Romance Writer thing, and see the real me …"

Jules frowned. "I have been trying to do that. Haven't I? At least, I thought I had."

"Well, good – but, Jules –"

And oh, how very much Jules wanted to know what Ewan was about to say then. Ewan Byge was sitting opposite him, with the most yearning, vulnerable look on his face, as if about to ask for the moon and the stars. And of course Jules would have gladly gone to fetch said items and given them to Ewan with a full heart. But –

"Fuckin' hell," came a new voice, rough as gravel. "It's the queers. Don't you two make a pretty pair?"

Jules looked up to find the Bad Guy looming over their table, arms crossed and expression belligerent. Two of his friends – whom Jules recognised from the courtroom's public gallery – stood at his shoulders. And they didn't look like entirely uncivilised sorts, but each one of them seemed bigger and meaner than Jules and Ewan put together on their very worst days.

"I tell you, if I'd known what sort of crap this bloke writes, I'd never have used him in the scam."

Ewan's words seemed to have failed him. He sat there looking pale with eyes and mouth wide.

"*Queer* romance? What the everlasting fuck?!" And the Bad Guy stepped forward to plant both fists – *thud* – on the flimsy table, and he leaned in threateningly –

"Oh *fuck* no," Ewan muttered. And suddenly he had stood up and dashed off in the opposite direction, disappearing around the corner as if all the hounds of hell were chasing him.

Jules stared after him, rather nonplussed to say the least.

It seemed the Bad Guy felt much the same way. After a moment, he hooted with laughter. "Well, mate," he said rather chummily to Jules, "queer or not, I think you're better off without that one."

Jules had to clear his throat, but he found his voice and replied, "I hope you're wrong." He sighed, and looked up at the man. "But I'm beginning to suspect you're right."

A lift of the chin acknowledged this, and the Bad Guy stepped away. "See ya back in there, then."

"See you," said Jules.

And he just sat there alone in the cool sunshine, and he quaked for a while, until eventually he decided his legs weren't too wobbly to walk after all.

Jules went into the pub to pay for their uneaten lunch, and then headed back to the court, where he sat on his own in the public gallery. The time dragged by, until at last the Bad Guy's name was called, and the sentence was read out. He was given no jail time, but he was required to pay a large fine, perform a really large amount of unpaid work in the community – and the victims were all to be compensated for the money they'd lost. Jules' name was listed, along with his six hundred and thirty pounds. It didn't seem all that important any more, and even now Jules didn't really expect to ever see that cash coming back to him. The Bad Guy couldn't pay what he didn't have, could he? It seemed unlikely that he'd be the sensible sort who had a savings account. But justice had been done, and Jules had seen it done. He eventually stood, nodded respectfully to the magistrates, and walked out of there in a morose mood.

He'd lost more than money now, hadn't he?

Jules had turned off his phone while he was in court, of course, and he didn't remember to turn it back on again until he was home. There was a missed call from Ewan, and a voicemail waiting for him which was presumably also from Ewan. Jules stared down at the notification, wondering if he even wanted to know. But finally he played it.

'Jules ... oh, Jules, I am so sorry I abandoned you, mate.' Which would have meant more if Ewan's tone wasn't all suppressed amusement. Apparently he thought he was just the funniest thing. 'I hope you're okay. I mean, I'm sure you are, but ... Look, I'm still your client, right? And I hope you're still my reader. I really hope you don't want anything more. I'd been trying to do the right thing and warn you off me, hadn't I? And now you know why. I'm sorry, Jules. It's shameful, I know, but I'm afraid I love me best of all.'

Jules sat there in the living room, staring at his phone while *The One Show* played out on the television with the sound muted. Jules obviously had some serious thinking to do. Which was a pity, seeing as his mind was just a complete woolly blank.

When Jem finally arrived home, she immediately saw something was wrong. She collapsed down beside him on the sofa, and asked, "Why so down at mouth, my sweet Jules?"

He grimaced at his own failures of insight. "I've just realised you were right. Ewan Byge belongs in Slytherin."

"Any means to an end?"

"He's not a bad person. Slytherins aren't, necessarily. But he really only cares about himself."

Jem sighed. "I'm sorry, mate."

He looked at her. "How did you know? You hadn't even met him."

"A guess, I suppose. An unlucky guess."

There were footsteps and the slight creak of old wooden stairs, and Archie appeared from the basement. "Ah, good. Both of you home at last."

"Hey, Archie," said Jem.

"I've been home for a while, actually," said Jules.

Archie looked at him, all astonishment. "You've been very quiet. What's wrong, son?"

"I've just realised that Ewan Byge is the Wickham in this story."

Archie blinked, as if the name rang a bell but the context escaped him.

"You know, in *Pride and Prejudice*," Jules explained, "where Wickham is the guy who's plausible but wrong for Elizabeth."

"Ah." Archie tried to hide the fact that he was pleased. "I'm sorry, Jules." He thrust his hands into his trouser pockets, and wandered off and back as if pondering something. When he came close again, he dared to ask, "Does that mean that Leonard is the Darcy, then?"

"Oh God!" Jules protested. "I haven't even finished thinking about the first bit yet!"

Eleven

Archie was right, though. Of course. Jules' instincts had known as much for a while, and all he had to do now was admit it to himself. And then he had to convince himself that he was worthy. Jules was no Elizabeth Bennet, after all!

"Honestly," Jules said to Archie as they folded laundry on the Sunday afternoon. "I've been such an idiot. If Leonard was in his right mind, he'd think I was a complete loser!"

"But obviously you're not, son, and Leonard is a wise enough man to see it."

"You have to think well of me," Jules argued. "It's in the job description. You're my Dad."

"I am very proud of you, yes – but not without reason. You are yourself, Jules, and you continue being yourself no matter what knocks life sends your way. That takes great courage."

"You're always saying I'm brave, and all I can think of are the times when I was scared. Which has been quite a lot."

"Courage is feeling the fear and doing it anyway. You know that. Leonard knows it, too. I think he was very impressed by you admitting your mistakes and reporting the fraud."

Jules scowled a bit. "Well, it turns out I wasn't the only one! And two of the other victims actually stood up in court and talked about how it had affected them, too."

Archie reached a hand to rub at Jules' shoulder. "You're being very hard on yourself, son."

"Am I?"

"You're a good person. You've been good to Leonard. You've proved what a decent young man you are. You knew he cared about you, and you've tried to be his friend without encouraging him to want more than you could give."

Jules let out a sigh. Honestly, he wasn't worthy. Leonard had kept the faith this entire time. "He's got his feet on the ground. I'm some silly airy-fairy flibbertigibbet, and he's firmly planted in the earth. I love that about him. He's too good for me."

Archie was smiling, mostly happy but a tad wry. "You're a fair way to being in love with Leonard already, Jules."

"Am I? I spent all this time thinking I was in love with Ewan Byge. Oh God!" Jules double-facepalmed. "And Leonard cared about me so much that he kept trying to set me up with Ewan, because he knew that's what I wanted."

Archie nodded. "He's a good man, too."

"Yeah. Too good for me. And *this* time I know what I'm talking about."

"Now, that's enough of that, Jules. It's the nature of love to think the object is marvellous, and the subject isn't worthy. Especially in these early days. You'll just have to take my word for it that you deserve Leonard – and actually I even think that he deserves you, which I couldn't say about very many people at all."

"Thank you, Dad," Jules said in a very weak voice. "You've got all the answers, don't you?"

Archie smiled at him. "I suppose I've been thinking about this a great deal. No doubt more than you'd really want me to. And my reward is giving you a whole lot of good advice that you're already figuring out on your own."

"That's giving me far too much credit! But I suppose as long as one of us knows what the hell I'm doing …"

"Jules, I know that you'll be brave enough to make the right choices and act on them, and you'll have that Happy Ever After you've been yearning for."

But Jules just groaned a little.

On the following Wednesday morning, however, Jules dressed with particular care. He'd decided on ink blue trousers, a pale green shirt, and a dark marine-green jumper, along with his navy blue pea coat. He ensured his quiff of thick red hair was neatly arranged, if jauntily asymmetrical. And he worked through the day at the office with an increasing sense of nervous anticipation.

He could hardly comprehend his own shock, then, when he stepped out of the office's front door to see that the pavement was distinctly Leonard-less. Jules looked up and down the street, and across to where anyone would approach if they'd arrived by Tube. But the place remained completely lacking in anything even remotely Leonard-related.

What on earth was that about? Honestly, for two months now Leonard had always been here on the dot, waiting for Jules. And now on the Wednesday when it mattered most, Leonard had completely neglected his duty.

Jules waited around like a lame duck for about ten minutes, and then just in case he headed around to Mr Oakley's Coffee House. "Have you seen my friend Leonard this evening?" he asked Daniel.

"Not today, Jules," Daniel briskly replied. Then he looked properly at Jules, and abruptly became more concerned. "Aw, I'm sorry, mate. I didn't realise you cared that much."

"I don't think he realised, either. And I've been utterly clueless."

"Look, if he pops in, I'll tell him you were looking for him, all right?"

"Thanks, Daniel."

Jules dragged himself home alone, to be met with equally shocked faces from both Archie and Jem. "He didn't show," he explained miserably.

"So, call him!" Jem tartly replied.

"Yes, call him," Archie agreed. "Now is not the time to give up, son."

"What if it was only ever about the case?"

"You know it wasn't, Jules. It's hardly standard practice for a police officer to be meeting up with a victim or a witness on a weekly basis, right through to the trial."

Jules just stood there, dazed enough to be swaying in a non-existent wind. "Oh. Isn't it?"

"No, it isn't," Jem agreed. "Come on, Jules. He probably just thinks you've finally got it together with Ewan Byge. All you have to do is call him – or text him, even – and disabuse him of the notion."

"Meh," said Jules, feeling too sorry for himself to come up with any kind of reasonable plan at all.

He spent the next day working as diligently as he could in a bid for distraction. He remained in his pyjamas, though he had to admit to himself that for once it felt slovenly rather than comfortable. And he drank coffee, and he binged on comfort food.

Archie and Jem were both home in good time, so they ended up eating their macaroni and cheese on the sofa with their feet up while watching *The One Show*. The announcement of a story about LGBTQ liaison officers at least sparked a little interest in Jules. What he wasn't expecting was to see Leonard sitting on the guest sofa in full uniform, next to a female officer likewise, while Alex Jones introduced them as 'the newest LGBTQ liaison officers in the City of London Police'.

Jules just sat there gaping throughout the story, while the other two muttered things like "Marvellous stuff! Just marvellous!" and "Go, Leonard! Go, you good thing!" Jules hardly heard a word of the interview, but his vision was full of Leonard being a little bit bashful and a whole lot of charming, not to mention handsome in his no-nonsense way. He *listened*, Jules could see him *listening* to Alex and Matt and his colleague, and then he responded just perfectly, with quiet confidence. All the while that smile of his, often so subtle and repressed, was fully deployed. Leonard was obviously very happy about his new role. It was no doubt only wishful thinking on Jules' part that Leonard betrayed a hint of wistfulness every now and then.

As soon as the spot was over, Jem turned to Jules and urgently said, "You've got to go to him, Jules. *Right fuckin' now*."

"Come on, son. Up and at 'em!"

"But —" said Jules.

"You know exactly where he is," Jem insisted. "Go get some clothes on, and I'll call for a cab."

"But —" said Jules.

Archie asked, like it was breaking his heart, "Didn't you see how sad he is, Jules?"

"No, he was happy!" Jules protested. "Happy about the job!"

"His eyes were sad," Archie stubbornly insisted.

"It's a live show, right? He'll have gone already." Jules found that he was getting up from the sofa, though.

Jem was already sorting through her contacts list for the taxi company. "It's not like they'll throw him out the door right away. Come *on*, Jules!"

"Oh God," said Jules. But he was heading upstairs to his bedroom, where he threw on the nearest available clothes, shoved his feet into shoes, and grabbed his wallet and keys. He dashed down again to the hallway, and shrugged into his coat.

A message pinged into Jem's phone. "Taxi's here!" she called through from the living room.

"Go get him, son," cried Archie, "and bring him back home."

There was time enough during the journey to make him doubt his own sanity ten times over, but soon Jules was delivered to the BBC's Broadcasting House. The World piazza stretched out before him, and the old-and-new buildings rose around him – pretty with blue lights, yet daunting in size. He stood there on the pavement, not even venturing yet beyond the bollards, and gazed up as if at a citadel. The cabbie drove off and left him there.

Right … How the hell was he meant to find Leonard?

Jules headed for the main entrance at the far end of the piazza, and went inside. He pleaded his case to the security guard, but naturally the guard insisted that the course of True Love could not run smooth if it was going to try getting past him. Jules retreated out into the cold night air, and glanced about him. A coffee shop looked relatively welcoming off to one side of the piazza, and Jules wondered if Leonard might not have ended up inside for a drink before heading off to work or home … But then chances were that if Jules went inside to check, Leonard would end up being somewhere else.

What to do, what to do?

It was as Jules dilly-dallied in the middle of nowhere that Leonard finally appeared, coming out of the main entrance with a small group of others, including his colleague, laughing and talking away. Jules had never seen him so expansive. Almost, for one long horrible moment, Jules decided he really wasn't brave enough after all. Did *this* Leonard, so happy, so full of life, and so engaged with his fellow human beans – Did this particularly delightful Leonard really need or even want Jules?

Well, if he did, Jules was forced to quickly conclude, Jules would be the luckiest bastard in all of London. He shored up his faint heart, and stepped forward. "Leonard."

Leonard immediately turned towards Jules, and with two strides was standing before him, his companions all lingering curiously. "Jules. How very good to see you." They looked at each other for a moment, both of them wondering what to do, what to say.

Almost despite himself, Jules murmured, "I missed you yesterday."

"Oh, I'm sorry," Leonard said in simple yet heartfelt tones. His smile, however, blossomed. If he'd looked happy before, Leonard now looked like the happiest creature *ever* in the whole history of the world. "I didn't think you'd –" Instead of finishing that thought, Leonard half turned back towards the others. "This is … my friend, Jules Madigan. Someone I enjoy liaising with," he added a tad cheekily, and thank heavens Leonard wasn't the sort to waggle his eyebrows. Not that the others didn't get the idea.

"I *am* your friend," Jules said. "And I'll be your boyfriend, too, if you'll still have me."

Leonard looked at him searchingly, seriously. And then he took Jules' hand in his, and corrected himself. "This is my boyfriend, Jules Madigan, with whom I love liaising."

Which was met with happy laughter, and a few hearty claps on the back for Leonard, and his colleague saying, "Pleased to meet you at last, Jules."

"Pleased to meet you, too," Jules managed – but the others were already moving on, leaving Leonard to his fate, which Leonard didn't seem to mind in the slightest.

Leonard was looking at him, his gaze running over Jules's face and arms and torso and legs as if for the very first time, as if Leonard hadn't really allowed himself to look properly before. "Oh, Jules, I really thought you'd –" Again, he didn't finish the thought.

"I've been an idiot," Jules confessed, "so we can just blithely skate past all that stupidity, if you like."

"Never an idiot," Leonard countered, "and never stupid."

Jules grinned at him, and let that nonsense stand. "Dad said I'm to bring you home. If that wouldn't be too weird?"

"Not weird at all. I like your father very much. And Jem as well," Leonard thought to add.

A giggle burst out of Jules, which he tried to repress, because he thought that if he started laughing he'd never stop, he'd just keep pealing out his joy like the bells of London.

"I'm sorry I don't have a home I can take you to," Leonard was continuing. "It's not the done thing at the section house to have guests, and it's hardly a comfortable place, in any case."

"We could wander around town, and have a drink, and do 'first date' type things."

Leonard just looked at him. "I'd rather go home with you. If I may."

"You may indeed. Absolutely."

They caught a cab, partly because Jules had belatedly realised he was wearing mismatched shoes, and the Tube was just too well-lit to be able to get away with such fashion catastrophes. "I shall just die a little if your friends noticed. See, I was in my pyjamas while we were watching *The One Show*, and I just grabbed whatever was convenient as Jem pushed me out the door ..."

Leonard was not fazed in the slightest. "Of course I chose an *interesting* person to fall for. I don't mind people knowing that."

"I'm not even investigating what other interesting clothing choices I made."

A silence grew in which Leonard did *not* offer to investigate later ... His pursed lips and averted eyes gave him away, though. Jules laughed merrily, and Leonard clasped his hand tighter. They'd been holding hands this entire time. It was delightful.

Finally they got back home, and Leonard even managed to pay the driver without letting go of Jules; he pulled out his wallet, and rested it on his knee while dipping into it for a twenty pound note, which included a rather decent tip. They headed up the steps together and Jules managed to unlock the front door one-handed as well. Then they were inside in the warm, and they looked at each other and laughed, because of course they had to let go now or else remain in their coats all evening long.

Once they were down to indoor clothes, Leonard looked at Jules for a long moment. Jules sensed what he was thinking – it was indeed time for their first kiss – and why not now, seeing as they hadn't been interrupted yet? Jules tipped his head towards the back of the house. "I can hear the others in the kitchen, and they're too tactful to –"

Leonard had already stepped forward, and now he lifted both hands – one to lightly grasp Jules' shoulder and the other to shape itself to his nape – and he slowly leaned in and pressed his mouth to Jules'. A still moment held ... and then they were both moving, and the kiss became sweetly hungry ... and then Leonard wrapped both arms firmly around Jules' shoulders, and gathered him up close, and the two of them were about as passionate as they could be while standing fully clothed in a hallway.

"Oh God," Jules groaned when they finally broke apart. "That was *awesome*. How d'you learn to kiss so good?"

Leonard's hand slid down Jules' arm, and slipped trustingly into his hand again. He seemed a little dazed. "You are my ruthful man."

"Is that a good thing?"

"My ruthful man. I've been looking for you my whole life."

"So ... what is that again?"

"The opposite of ruthless. You are full of ruth. Kindness and compassion. You are so kind as to care for me."

"Oh, no ... that's more like enlightened self-interest, or something."

Leonard smiled, and seemed to reconnect with the everyday world. "Oh, Jules ..."

"Are we going to ... ?" Jules cleared his throat. "If I'm moving too fast, *please* just tell me, but will you stay the night? With me, I mean."

"Yes," Leonard said, his voice little more than a rough whisper, "I will."

"Good. Well, I mean excellent. Truly excellent. Okay." Jules sighed. "You'd better come through and say hello to Dad and Jem, but you should let me whisk you away just as soon as you can bear it."

"Yes."

"They won't think anything of it. I mean, they're probably staying out of the way now so as to let us choose. Not that they won't tease, but they won't mean anything by it."

"It's all right," said Leonard. "Let's go and say hello."

They walked into the kitchen hand in hand, although even without that it was no doubt perfectly obvious that they were finally together. Leonard was quietly, unselfconsciously happy, walking tall and kind of dazed as if in a dream. Jules knew he himself was just broadcasting a beatific glow on all channels.

Of course Archie and Jem looked them both over, and grinned. Archie stepped forward with his hand out, saying, "It's wonderful to see you again, Leonard. I'm very glad you came."

Luckily Leonard was holding Jules' right hand with his left, so he could shake hands with Archie without letting go of Jules. "I'm very glad to be here, sir. Mr Madigan. Archie. Sorry. It was good of you to invite me."

Archie chuckled. "Are you two hungry?" He was cutting a loaf of bread.

"We're making vegetable soup," Jem explained. "There's plenty. We figured you could reheat it later if you're not in the mood for anything now."

Leonard seemed to stoically ignore her wink, and looked to Jules for agreement before replying, "That would be very welcome, thank you. Perhaps only a small portion for me, though."

"I'm too happy to eat much!" Jules declared.

"Now, you two young men need your nourishment," Archie said with nary a blush nor a quaver. "So, sit down at the table, and we'll be dishing up shortly. I can't promise this is anything as good as what Jules would make, Leonard – he's the real chef of the family – but I trust it will be acceptable."

"I'm sure it will be wonderful, Archie."

"You could tell us about this new job of yours, if you feel like talking. We were so pleased to see your interview – you came across very well – and it seems to be the ideal role for you."

"Thank you, Archie. I'm very pleased about it myself."

"Excellent, excellent."

Archie fetched the butter, and Jem was bringing across the saucepan of soup and placing it on a trivet so that she could dish out at the table. Jules smiled to watch them; he'd trained them well. And this welcome for Leonard was the most marvellous thing … The completely unromantic Jem even buttered a couple of pieces of bread for Jules and Leonard so they needn't quit holding hands. They all laughed at how ridiculous the new couple were being, but then again no one expected or even wanted them to stop.

Jules managed about four or five spoonfuls of the soup – which was actually rather delicious – and half his piece of bread, before slowing to a halt. He just wasn't interested. Leonard was much the same. They sat there for a while, occasionally taking part in Archie and Jem's natterings about their respective days, their intentions for the weekend, and any other little thing that came into their heads. Or at least, Jules occasionally took part. Leonard stayed fairly quiet.

"I'm sorry, Leonard," Archie eventually said. "We must seem a bit much, when you're used to being on your own. I hope we're not overwhelming you."

Leonard smiled, though a little stiffly. "Even if you were, it wouldn't be unwelcome."

"That's kind of you to say."

After a moment, Leonard continued, "I talked to you before about how … independent my parents each were. Well, all my family. When I was younger, I used to marvel at my parents actually staying together all their lives. They would always be taking separate trips for this or that, they'd work or study in different places, they'd hardly even holiday together. It was … unsettling at times. But then I didn't exactly mind about travelling with first one and then the other. I saw a great deal of the world for a while, until they finally settled in London." He nodded a little, as if confirming old memories. "I didn't really appreciate it until later on, but they were never not … together. They had such a strong bond, as partners."

When it seemed clear that Leonard had finished for now, Archie said lightly, "What an interesting life you've lived, Leonard!"

Leonard nodded again in acknowledgement, and then continued. "I want a strong bond like that, in my life, with my partner." His hand tightened around Jules' hand. "But I would also like to be together, as well as together – if you see what I mean." A small wry smile twisted his lips. "Which is really just a very long way of saying thank you, Archie, none of this is unwelcome."

"I'm very glad," said Archie, looking a bit damp around the eyes. "I'm really very glad you're here with us, Leonard. I don't think Jules could have found a finer fellow."

And what more could anyone say? Leonard had in effect declared his intentions, and Archie had in effect given his blessing. Jules, for once, was lost for words, and maybe none were needed. Even Jem was looking a tad sentimental.

Jules stood, and tugged at Leonard's hand so that he stood, too. "Thanks, Dad," Jules said, leaning in to press a kiss to Archie's cheek. "We'll see you in the morning. Goodnight, Jem. Thanks for the soup."

"My pleasure, Jules babe. Goodnight, Leonard."

"Goodnight, ma'am," Leonard replied without seeming at all aware of it.

Jules turned away with a smile, and led Leonard up the stairs to his bedroom.

The two of them were quiet once they were alone in the room with the door closed. There was a mixed sensation of both peace and anticipation. It felt utterly right that they were here together. And they were both yearning for what came next, though it seemed that neither of them wanted to rush it.

They kind of came adrift at last, and Leonard wandered about, looking at all the bits and bobs that probably conveyed all there was to be told about Jules Madigan. At some point, of course, he came to the ornate silver frame hanging on the wall, and the manuscript page which may or may not have been the genuine article.

"I'm sorry." Jules slid past him, and put hands on the frame, intending to take it down. "I should have been rid of this ages ago."

"No," Leonard immediately responded. "No, leave it. Please. Unless you really can't bear it."

Jules didn't turn, but asked over his shoulder, "Why would you want it on display?"

"Because if you hadn't bought that, we might never have met."

Understanding dawned on him. "Oh … It's Dexter and Mike's Happy Ever After – and it's the Once Upon a Time of *our* story."

"Just so," said Leonard.

Leonard sat down on the side of the bed, and Jules went to stand in the V of his thighs. Leonard was gazing up at him full of yearning, and his hands were firm at Jules' waist … and yet somehow it wasn't quite time to kiss. Jules rested his hands on Leonard's shoulders, and smiled softly. "I have to ask you what Elizabeth Bennet asked Mr Darcy."

"What would that be?" Leonard asked, echoing Jules' own unrushed tones.

"She wanted to know how he could ever have fallen in love with her. She couldn't understand how it began. 'What set you off in the first place?'"

Leonard grinned, and his arms wrapped themselves around Jules with undemanding comfort. "I was intrigued before I'd even met you. Your emails, Jules, and the evidence you'd compiled – they were like nothing I'd ever read before. Certainly not in that context."

"Oh!" That was an unexpected answer. "They were just ordinary emails."

"No," Leonard said with a shake of his head. "You were always thoughtful, despite the difficult situation. You were clever and resourceful. And you were kinder than you had any need to be, to everyone involved."

"Oh my God. Wasn't I a crashing disappointment when you finally met me?"

"Not at all. At first ... Well, I know you'll argue with me, but you're *beautiful*, Jules. And you're – forgive me – you're *colourful*. Not just your hair, but how you dress, how you behave. Everything about you is ... so full of life."

Jules was absolutely lost for words, though he stuttered out, "No, I –"

"You engaged me, right from when you walked down the steps from your office. Maybe for shallow reasons at first. But as I got to know you, even that evening as I took your statement, I realised my first impressions hadn't been wrong. You were so different to anyone else I'd ever met. You're a good man, Jules. My ruthful man. It didn't take me long to realise I'd found you at last."

"Oh ..." was all Jules could manage, but with that luxurious groan he gave all of himself.

Leonard was looking up at him with utter trust. Even now, he was willing and wanting, but not demanding, not insisting. Jules ran his hands over the warm dark night of Leonard's hair, pushed fingertips through the star-shimmer at his temples – and then Jules let his palms cup Leonard's face, before finally leaning in to kiss him.

The kiss was even more magical than before. Already they were getting a feel for each other's rhythms and desires. Leonard strengthened his embrace around Jules' waist, and pulled him in close so that Jules was delightfully off-balance.

They kissed and their hands tentatively began exploring further, until they couldn't bear not to be doing more. Which didn't take all that long, really.

Jules regained his footing, and stepped back. Leonard stood. And then somehow they drifted apart again, and each of them undressed himself while watching the other, until at last they were both standing there naked. At first Leonard almost stood to attention – in posture, at least – as if being inspected. But after a moment or two he relaxed, and even seemed to like that they should finally after all this while be their own true selves with each other, nothing more and nothing less. If Jules had known ahead of time they'd be doing it this way, he would have assumed it would be excruciatingly embarrassing, but actually it was rather profound.

Leonard did indeed have the wiry runner's body that Jules had anticipated. And he was a sweet light olive all over, though his arms and legs were darker, as if he wore shorts and a t-shirt when running. "How splendid you are!" Jules said.

"You're lovely, Jules, inside and out."

"You're lovelier."

Leonard shook his head, and laughed. "I know you hate it when you blush, Jules, but I love being able to see you so clearly. Someone once told me you're an open book, and I love that about you."

To be so simple and easily seen through didn't necessarily strike Jules as such a great thing.

Leonard's laughter quietened, but didn't disappear. "Sometimes I find you a bit contrary when I'm trying to pay you compliments, though."

"Maybe ..." Jules said, turning away in order to tug the bulk of the duvet down to the foot of the bed. "Maybe ..." he murmured, holding out his hand. "Maybe it's time for us both to show and not tell."

"Yes," Leonard agreed in a whisper. When he walked over to take Jules' hand, Jules got onto the bed, shuffling back and drawing Leonard after him – Leonard, who followed with a relieved sigh as if to say 'At last'.

Jules brought him closer still, and then took the man into his arms – gathering him up, as Leonard gathered him – so they were lying on their sides facing each other, Jules propped on his elbow so he could lean in and initiate another kiss. An involving, passionate kiss, with Leonard clutching him up even closer as if he'd been waiting for this, yearning for this, for so very long now.

Leonard was fantastic at kissing, or maybe they were fantastic at kissing each other. Jules happily kept that going while his free hand slowly stroked its way down Leonard's long sinewy back. Eventually, as things were heating up rather, Jules shaped his palm to a narrow buttock, letting his fingertips delve a little deeper, and he hauled Leonard closer still so they were mashed up tight together. He started the slightest slowest roll of his hips so they rubbed together – dry, like matches about to light a fire.

Leonard shuddered a little and muttered "Oh fuck", which was the first time Jules had ever heard Leonard swear. Jules grinned and broke their kiss so he could lift his head and look at the man. Leonard was already in the zone, his dark eyes hot and unfocused. "Oh Jules ... oh fuck ... please ..."

Jules obliged him, thrusting hard once, twice – and abruptly Jules was in the zone as well, and he found himself rutting against Leonard, his hand unrelentingly holding the man right where he wanted him, and they were mouthing mad kisses, a mutual madness. Leonard's arms twisting tighter, his fingers digging in, and his mouth ravenous.

Then without any warning Leonard was coming, and a sharp cry became a grateful moan as he quaked in Jules' arms. Once he was done, Jules pushed him over a little further and thrust himself against Leonard's deliciously sticky-wet skin until moments later he came, too, with something like a satisfied chuckle escaping him and then a groan as grateful as Leonard's.

They stayed there tightly bound up together for long moments while the world slowly righted itself about them. Then finally they eased apart, and comfortably back together again.

"Thank you, Jules," Leonard said, quietly yet meaning it, Oh My God *meaning it*.

Jules did chuckle then, from pure joy. "It was my pleasure, too, if you didn't notice. Thank *you*, Leonard." They were both so utterly relaxed, but before Jules reached for the duvet he whispered into the hush, "D'you wanna clean up?"

Leonard laughed a little, under his breath. "It's your bed, so you should decide. But I've never felt happier to be rather a mess."

Well, that settled that! Jules drew up the duvet and they eased closer still, as if they belonged together, as if they were each the perfect shape for the other to fit with. Jules smiled, and sighed. "Are we going to have a Happy Ever After, then?"

"We're going to bloody well try," Leonard replied rather fiercely.

Jules grinned as his heart soared. "The End."

"Oh, Jules, my ruthful man," said Leonard, as if talking about something truly marvellous. "It's only the beginning – and as beginnings go, I think it's brilliant."

About Julie Bozza

I was born in England and lived most of my life in Australia before returning to the UK a few years ago; my dual nationality means that I am often a bit too cheeky, but will always apologize for it.

I have been writing fiction for almost thirty years, mostly for the enjoyment of myself and my friends, but writing is my love and my vocation so of course that's where my dreams and ambitions are. In the meantime, technical writing helps to pay the mortgage, while I also have fun with web design, reading, watching movies and television, knitting, and imbibing espresso.

If you would like to know more, please come and join the conversation at my blog juliebozza.com or on Twitter twitter.com/juliebozza

Other titles by Julie

The Definitive Albert J. Sterne
Homosapien … a fantasy about pro wrestling
The Valley of the Shadow of Death
Albert J. Sterne: Future Bright, Past Imperfect
Butterfly Hunter
The Fine Point of His Soul
The Apothecary's Garden
Of Dreams and Ceremonies
A Threefold Cord
The Thousand Smiles of Nicholas Goring
Mitch Rebecki Gets a Life
A Pride of Poppies (anthology)

51877546R00075

Made in the USA
Charleston, SC
06 February 2016